ESCAPE FROM MICTLÁN

WILL LORIMER

INKISTAN
.COM

1

WALPURGIS NIGHT
AT THE CANTINA

Thirteen o'clock, and everything had changed in the Town with no name. Come again? Since my departure certain facts had altered. Take that   sign above the hotel door, repainted with a double-headed hawk and the legend, '*la Houff del Halcon*' – an unhappy marriage of Gothic and Spanish – and below that, '*Prop. R. Von Hapsburg*'. A familiar name, though I couldn't quite place it. The new owner, I supposed, standing in the open door, absurd as only aristos ever can be, clad in lederhosen britches and poncho, matching houndstooth tweed, a surfeit of pork pies in a florid face framed by bugger-lug sideburns almost but not quite meeting in a beard; native lads jumping to his barked commands, porting tottering stacks of boxes into the lit-up hotel.

At the street corner, where a steep lane ran down one side of the old stone building, tethered to the wall, nine or ten *burros* contentedly munching hay, their comingled breaths steaming in the cold night air. Looked like the party had just arrived. Not a good moment, I thought gloomily, not a good moment at all.

Mañana? And so soon? 'Hey, *gringo*[1], plenty room at this

---

[1] Gringo, sometimes used derogatively, derived either from *Grigo*, the Greek word for stranger, or from the Scottish song 'Green Grow the Rushes O', which was a favourite of the Texas Rangers, during the Mexican-US war 1846-1868, when Mexico lost a third of its territory to the U.S.

inn!' At least someone hadn't changed while I was away. Across the street, Cantina Joe, all polished smiles and practised bonhomie, waving us over. His hole-in-the-wall bar heaving this Walpurgis Night.

'Not a good idea,' I whispered, grabbing Jaime's arm as he started forwards.

'Is my risk,' Jaime replied, taking the opportunity to freshen up his lipstick. 'I do not need protecting in this town, my *generalísmo*,' he said, hitching up his suspenders, and smoothing out the wrinkles of his lurex mini skirt.

An ambuscade of wolf whistles as he pushed through half doors, reminding me of Jaime's recent change of sex. That was my friend the *borracho* fuckers' slime-balls were ogling! Ten sombreros camped around a mariachi wearing cactus headgear, playing a *narcocorida polka* on a yamaha keyboard in the far corner. Rotating chairs, raising glasses, smacking lips like they already had the taste of her. Cherry kissers pouting back as Jaime returned the compliment to thunderous approval. This was a men-only *cantina*. Dangerous territory for a *muchacha* on the run – more so if that *muchacha* was Mexico's most notorious narco-traficante with a five million peso reward on his head.

'Easy *hombres!*' Joe boomed over the heel stamping din. 'Enough!' he yelled, manoeuvring his great belly behind the narrow bar, pushing up denim shirt sleeves up his hairy arms, grinning like a busted honky-tonk, leaning on the counter. 'My friend, you look like hell,' he rasped. 'What you been doing?' He tilted his chin, 'Climbing the skirts of *las tres hermanitas?*'

'No. I mean, yes,' I muttered, slumping with exhaustion from our long climb up the mountain to the town.

'What you do then? Rescue this *muchacha* from a *barrancha*?' he grinned, rolling his 'r's like balls in a bowling alley.

'A ravine is right!' I snapped out of my slump. 'Are you going to serve us or what? We're bloody freezing.'

'*Mezcal?*'

'*Cómo no?*' Jaime leant an arm on my shoulder. 'I see you have my favourite.' She pointed a red varnished finger nail. 'Up there, on the top shelf, *el gusano del diablo.*'

'So, you are *not* a total stranger,' Joe said, reaching for an unlabelled brown bottle.

'My friend,' Jaime said, 'I am born in these mountains.'

'Where exactly?' Joe replied, sliding two brimming glasses, sans worm, along the polished bar.

'What's with all the questions, Joe?' I demanded, slopping *mezcal* in my haste to drink up and get the fuck out.

'Is ok,' Jaime murmured in my ear. 'I can look after myself.'

'I am only being friendly,' Joe shrugged, reaching under the bar, for a cloth rather than the sawn-off shotgun I knew he kept there.

'I tell you anyway, for I am feeling generous tonight,' Jaime said, as Joe refilled my empty glass, 'A little village, higher in the mountains. Maybe you even know it, Santa Domingo del Flores? I never forget, though it is a long time.'

'*Sí,* I know it well. I have a brother in that village,' Joe nodded, mock serious. 'But never there do I see there such a *bonita muchacha.*'

'That is because I am wearing *pantalonés* the last time you visit.' Jaime leaned closer. 'Do not you recognise me *oncle?*'

'Jaime!' Joe gasped. '*¿Qué pasa?* Why you dressed like this?'

'Not so loud,' Jaime hissed, eyeing the angle-on sombreros.

7

'Is this real?' I growled, turning to look at both in turn. 'Joe, are you everyone's uncle round here?'

'You are in Mexico, my friend,' Joe grinned, hand on heart. 'Here big families *es* normal. I can count on a hundred and thirty-two in mine, brothers to second cousins. And all can count on me.' He hesitated. '*Es* why I have to talk with Jaime,' he shrugged, apologetically, '*En privado*.'

'Yea, sure,' I said, downing my second mezcal, breaking out in a sweat as I stood up. 'Plenty of room at the inn, huh?'

'Sit down, my foolish young friend.' Joe flapped a hand at my vacated barstool, 'I read the reports in newspapers las Malinchés bring me,' 'But only after *she* reads them first.' He thumbed to the lit-up hotel, outside. 'So, you can count on it, she knows about the reward. That bruja and Gomez,' he pincered thumb and forefinger, 'They are *this* close.' He chuckled. 'I tell you, cross the street and you lead my nephew straight into a trap.' Glancing round, he nodded at the sombreros in the corner, whispering amongst themselves. 'All Jaime's cousins,' he grinned, 'Even if he does not recognise them!' Drawing himself up, he thumped a fist on the counter. 'In my family *es* the same as brother. Blood so thick, *es* better than any superglue.'

2

A LIKELY TALE

So Jaime had a team. I was glad for him. A posse of cousins, good as brothers ... better even, since superglue had entered the equation. So where did that leave his generalísimo? Out in the cold, lingering by the Cantina's half doors watching the handshakes and backslapping within - turning to face my mother, the only family I had. All she had to offer, by way of affection, a one-way ticket on the long slide. No return? How many times had I told myself that? But I was returning. Not so much because I didn't have anywhere else to go; more like living the life preordained. My every moment already entered in a book. Hell? I was half way there already, hurtling hot rails. Way to go! But, perversely, maybe knowing I was foredoomed freed me? For then I was also ...

'Free, to do what the fuck I want.' Singing that to the narcocorrida polka playing in the cantina at my back, I stepped jauntily across the street, heading for the bruja's lair.

But wasn't I forgetting someone? Herr Fucking Hapsburg, occupying the doorway. That was my light he was blocking. A palm upraised, a pork pie so presented. 'I'm afraid the hotel is closed.'

Same old song, same old story. I was about to shoulder the porcine fuck aside, when Helga loomed at his back.

'Not to worry,' she breathed, nuzzling her chin on his shoulder, her great hands clasped over his barrel chest, rocking him back and forth. 'Quinton, this is my old pal Rudy from Brussels, he buys the hotel for me, is not that wunderba?'

'Wonderbra!' I recycled, realising my trip to the plain had all along, been a ploy. 'So,' I glared at him, 'Why'd you arrive by burro train,' I nodded at the donkeys, 'When it's so much easier to come by bus?'

'Excellent question,' Herr Rudy Fucking Hapsburg smiled patronisingly. 'That is because tomorrow, or rather later this morning, if all goes to plan,' ostentatiously, he glanced down at the luminous face of his soup plate sized Patek Philippe five-dials gold chronometer on his wrist, 'At five o'clock sharp, we set off on an expedition into uncharted territory.'

'Better we continue this inside,' Helga whispered, glancing to either side. 'The street it is so naked.'

Following the gross, disproportionately sized – her height and his girth – arm-in-arm lovers into the hotel lobby, I hung back as they turned the corridor towards the salon, reassured to find the old retainer was still propped against the wall. Maybe the shrivelled mummy in the rusting suit of Conquistador armour really was the corpse of my father, I reflected, pausing to adjust the helmet, oddly comforted by the empty sockets staring blindly back. His continued presence a good sign, I considered, suggesting that, even this Walpurgis Night, some things were not subject to change.

Then, when I got back to my room, the basket of peyote buttons was still on the bedside table where I left it, back in my room. Yes, with the altitude my toothache had returned with a vengeance, but not for long I reassured myself, packing a double dose of buttons between my gums and my teeth – for good measure pocketing a handful, so as not to be caught short later.

The salon was now decorated with bunting, as if for a homecoming. A blazing fire in the grate, and pride of place above the mantelpiece, a gold-framed daguerreotype of a certain Maximillian. Even I knew of the last emperor of Mexico, archduke of Austria and dupe of Napoleon III, but there was something familiar about the face, those absurd sideburns, almost but not quite meeting in a beard. And then I made the connection – of course he was a Hapsburg, just like the Baron of Bacon, before me.

'Excellent,' Rudy snorted, turning to smile at Helga, sitting pretty on the sofa beside him. 'What do I tell you?' He patted her broad hand resting on his fat knee. 'Never I am wrong with first impressions.' Pink piggy eyes swivelled my way. 'Quinton, you must join our quest.'

'Quest?' I grinned, standing with my back to the fire, 'That implies a prize.'

'You will share the spoils, that I promise.' Rudy boomed.

'So what's it all about, this, um ... expedition?'

Rudy waved at the portrait. 'The same purpose that brought my great-great uncle here,' he faltered, 'To his tragic death.'

'Really?' I said. 'If you don't mind me saying, I thought Maximillian was the dupe of Napoleon III and his ambitions for French global domination.'

'The historians have it wrong.' Rudy shook his head, 'True, Napoleon ultimately put Maximillian on the eagle throne, but that was down to the plotting of Carlota and it gave Napoleon the excuse he needed to get rid of her. She hated sea voyages, you must understand, and wouldn't have come otherwise.'

'So,' I said, taking the seat opposite, 'What was your great uncle's true reason?'

'Ah!' Rudy let out a splendid sigh. 'Thereby hangs a tale. It all started when Maximillian opened the crypt of my ancestor

Rudolph, the holy Roman emperor, and discovered a very strange cache of bones sharing his tomb.' He paused, for effect, 'Rudolph was the first Hapsburg to win the purple robe, an honour, incidentally, that he shared with Julius Caesar. Hapsburg means "houff of the hawk".' His beady eyes twinkled. 'You may have noticed the little sign outside I put above the door?'

'Two heads are better than one eh?' I smiled. 'Beats having eyes at the back of your head.'

'Yes, of course,' Rudy muttered, distractedly.

'When one sleeps, the other wakes.' I went on. 'As a logo for a hotel, I would have thought it's a bit schizo. But perhaps that's the point?'

Rudy turned again to Helga, impassive at his side. 'Your friend may be perceptive.' He waggled a finger. 'But not perceptive enough.'

'So what then am I missing?' I held up a hand, 'Let me guess, the hawk isn't really a hawk. Yes, I can see it now,' I said, staring at a point above Rudy's left shoulder, 'flapping leathery wings over las tres hermanitas, coming closer now, those two heads by a trick of distance, merging into one great ugly head with a cranial bump of cartilage at the back, giving the impression it is looking both ways. It's a pterodactyl! Yes, beyond doubt, not just a large zopilote. That's a vulture, you understand,' I added, folding my arms.

I wasn't prepared for the stunned silence as they exchanged glances; denial in hers.

'Oh my friend,' at last Rudy said. 'You are my friend, you know. Until my monogram on the subject was privately circulated,' he raised a fat finger, 'But only, you understand, to the members of my club, no one else but Maximillian and myself fits the pieces of the puzzle together.' He sighed. 'With your insight, I probably don't have to tell you these the unmapped mountains are the last hiding place of the ancient pterodactyl.'

'Indubitably,' I nodded, keeping my face straight with an effort.

'Of course, in their ignorance, the local Indians call the flying dinosaur the tzitzimime. Why?'

I shook my head to clear it, but I needn't have bothered straining for an answer, for the Baron's question was merely rhetorical.

'Yes,' he continued, 'It most often seen in storms when lightning strikes the peaks. The Indians believe it is the double of thunder. And because it higher than any other bird, they also believe that the tzitzimime is the nagual of the highest god.' He paused ponderously. 'It is this aspect that for me makes the death of Maximilian more bearable.'

'Pardon me, Baron,' I interjected slyly, 'Surely Maximillian was executed by firing squad at Quertaro?'

'No,' Rudy shook his flaccid jowls, 'That was the story Presidenté Juarez put out to please Yankee public opinion.'

'Really?' I frowned, reaching into my hip pocket for a top-up of peyote, to better cogitate on this.

'Yes,' he nodded, 'Juarez was an Indian and so understood the concept of honour, though as a Republican, obviously he fought on the wrong side. Maximillian was accorded the same rights as the ancient Tolucan kings, who, by their custom, ruled for a year and a day. He was offered up to the sun with his many medals and staked out on a mountain ledge to wait for the nagual of Amomati, the highest god. Despite the drugs they gave him, it was a terrible death. That is the reason for my quest. To rescue his precious bones.'

Rudy lofted that finger heavenwards. 'I have seen for myself the eyrie on the mountain they call la Tercer Hija de la Noché – the third daughter of night – on an inaccessible crag, close to the summit. He is there, I swear, along with all the lesser kings and their Indian treasure, gold enough to attract the nagual of the highest god, who, in the burning light of midday, confuses the gilded sacrifice for the glare of the sun. Enough, I promise to keep you in luxury for the rest of your life, if that is what you desire. For myself,' he sighed, laying a hand on his chest, 'The bones will be enough. Like Maximilian, I have no need for worldly wealth.'

Is that so, I thought, Herr Fucksburg, all right for you, with your ancestral crypt, and hedge funds bordering rolling hectares of your country pile, and your hereditary membership of an elite Brussels club, slurping golden shit till the cows come home. Some of us have to work for a living. Of course, I wasn't including myself, I'd never pay off the loans accrued in my student days, not without a degree or the inclination. But, before I flunked out, at least I had researched this shit about nagualism, naguals and doubles, and that was one subject in which the Baron of Bacon couldn't pull a blind on me.

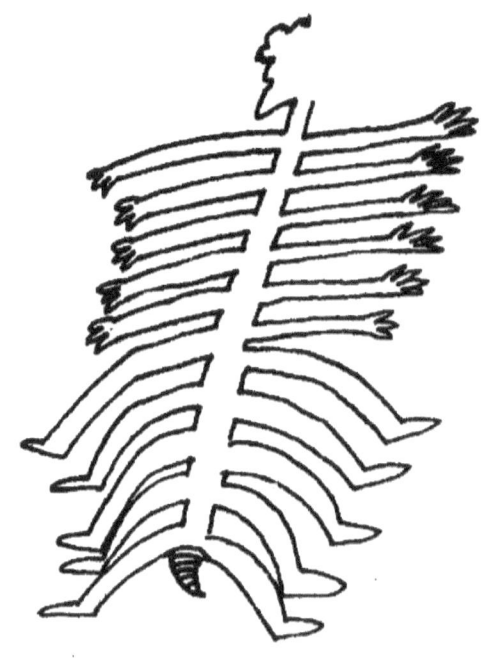

3

THE MATING DANCE OF THE GIANT
MILLIPEDE

It was time – by the luminous dial of my fake Rolex – five in the morning, but still no sign of Herr Hapsburg. I'd awoken with a throbbing hard-on, perhaps brought about by all the bumping below my bed. When I looked down, two boys bolted for the door, giggling as they ran. Fully roused now, I wondered if somehow I had turned the wrong page and woken up in a Jean Austin novel, but no; this was no sassy Western, about lariats and lynching, this was seamy-side Mexico, those boys had been 'nekked', as Ms. Austin might have said, one hard on the heels of the other, not to mention two pairs of reddened buttocks. Rum goings-on obviously. I wondered what Herr Hapsburg's real purpose was for mounting his expedition? Those boys were barely into their teens. So why did he want me along? Perhaps he was afraid of the mountain Indians and discovery. Certainly a lot of cacti to hang his *cojones* on, out in purple sage badlands. And the worst of it was, even though I'd also come up with it myself, I'd almost believed the story about the pterodactyl. Though my annoyance was chiefly at myself, I resolved to tell the Belgian shite-eater where to stuff it, but only after I had caught up on some sleep.

I hadn't counted on a Malinché sister – which one? I didn't know – disturbing my repose, slipping into the bedroom when my back was turned. No lock on the door you see, so easy to come and go in that renamed hotel.

Was this a test? Helga, I was sure, somewhere in the background, putting her up to it. Or perhaps this was my reward for stringing Herr Hapsburg along? In either case I didn't care. I was hard, rock hard, the blood all gone from my head to my dick and balls, which seemed to have sprouted wings. I was flying. But by *Jésu*, she was a hot *tortilla*, and I was the *salsa*. No sour looks from her pussy when I got up close. But then sheets wafted up again, letting in more than the draft and I was seeing double – no, triplicate, as a third Malinché sister came to join the show. Was this late entry her nagual, and the second one her double, I wondered absently. lost in the moment, identical faces swimming out of velvet dark, hard to tell how many hands, bumps and curves. Native American skin, warm leatherette wrapping me in a multi-tentacular suction embrace, my half-baked whiteness and colonialist guilt expunged at last, my only worry when I rolled over the bed might not be big enough and, like the nursery rhyme, one of us might fall out. However, I need not have worried, for the three girls, obviously well used to working as a team, had everything under control, except the lead in my pencil, which I did, saving it up till I came with an enormous detonation that quite cleared my brain, and then we did it again, and again. Hey *cabrón*, I was riding high, until outside the shutters a cock crowed and it was time for the girls to go. Yes, I had it confirmed, triplets. Life would never be the same again. The strangest being ever I encountered. One face, with a multi-tentacular liposuction embrace. That was *me*; the weird sisters were stealing away without the door, sperm enough to start a nation. Little half-casts with cheery grins. *Alto Anglo*, from *la nueva república delas sierras*. My contribution to the melting-pot of the Americas.

4
HEAD-START

Too late ... Never too late ... Always too late ... Way too late ... Conflicting voices in my head, and still I didn't get the message. What message? Thuds and bangs out there. Dragging sounds. Barked commands. Muffled giggling – a lot of that. Couldn't they stop? And then they did. All quiet on the Western Front. The big guns gone silent. Just the whoosh of leathery wings, swooping down on the cream of the crop, the dead and the dying stiffening in the mud. Flanders? No ...

And there they were again, as I found upon entering the dining room, among food debris and plates, hand-drawn pterodactyls on menus I hadn't seen before, swooping down on a cartoon expeditionary force, wending the three little sisters. On the inside pages, the dishes on offer, 'Tortillas pterodáctilas con enchantas', surely that meant enchiladas? 'Tostadas pterodáctilas con queso del muerto ...' – the cheese of death? Was I still off my face on peyote and hallucinating all this? But no, that breakfast menu was real, and was headed by 'Houff del Halcon,' gothic script, above the salutation ... 'Adalante Rudy!' Onwards and upwards, I supposed it meant, and, beside that, a passable caricature of Herr Hapsburg wearing a crown.

'You like?' Helga breathed, from above my head.

Scary? I'll say! That mother just materialised.

'I makes that while you are screwing your sisters.'

'My sisters?' I repeated, twisting round, and regarding her blankly.

'You know perfectly well,' she said, grinning like a

demented cheshire cat. '*Las Malinchés!*'

'What, me?' I blinked, a memory popping into mind of a childhood game of ring a ring of roses, with my kid sisters in the attic of the old Presbytery.

'Do not insult me with denials,' she scowled, towering like a column of black smoke. 'I know what it is you do with them in your room.

'You do?' I echoed.

'Yesss!' she hissed. 'And the worst of all is your lies.'

'Oh those!' I said, 'I can't help it.' I shrugged, 'A congenital condition, it runs in the family.'

'Ach!' She clawed her brow. 'Why are so maddening? Do you think you are the apple pip in my eye? I must be out my skull to put ups with you. And you pay nothing for board! What exactly is it you wants?'

'Treasure!' I grinned, wondering what sort of mum would have his triplet half-sisters bed him. 'Or have you forgotten? I waggled a finger. 'We have a deal!'

'I am not so sure,' she snarled. 'Now I owns the hotel again, what is the hurry?'

'So Gomez was right,' I glared. 'You owned it before.'

'Yes, Quinton,' she said, implacable as a stone goddess.

'And now you've bought it back.'

'Wrong,' she smiled, evilly. 'I get it as a present. Rudy signs the paper before he leaves. What is the hotel to him,' she shrugged, 'When he has the treasures of an empire. You know the fat fool thinks he returns wearing the crown of Mexico.'

'You have got to be joking,' I said, half convinced she was putting me on. 'He is really that *loco?*'

'Yes, my son!' she leered like a crocodile, lazing on mudbanks, the growing gulf between us, a wide turgid river.

24

'Is in the blue blood, my son. All those European royals related. Too much bumping about in stately carriages, that is why! Incest!' she said, derisively. 'Makes you weak in the head.'

5
BACK IN THE CANTINA

Cantina Joe! In my hour of need, who else could I call on this *siesta* time? Jaime, wherever he was, I supposed, but Joe wasn't letting on, fingers patrolling the counter, marshalling sugar crystals spilled en route to my cup. The coffee, scalding hot, black and treacly, and 'on the *casa!*' Perhaps Joe was independently rich, he could even be the drugs cartel banker, this none-too-clean bar his preferred way of passing the time, luring ne'er-do-wells into idle conversation. No one else around, barring that dusty *caballero*, walked in from the Kalahari by the looks of him, dead to the world in the corner, presenting holed soles, boots propped on the cold stove, staring vacantly over half doors at the deserted street. Maybe he really was dead, I considered, chewing meditatively on a wad of peyote, as was now habitual, watching a bar fly emerge from the gaping cavern of his mouth, grubbing feet, before buzzing off to pastures new.

'You are saying?' Joe, prompted.

'Was I?' I frowned, wondering whether I had mentioned my second *intimation*, and Helga's cancer, 'Sorry, I can't remember.'

'The new owner of the hotel?' Joe said, indulgently.

'Oh yea. That crazy Herr Hapsburg. Packed up and offski early this morning.' I sighed, 'If I hadn't slept in, I might have tagged along.'

'I hear 'bout that,' Joe said absently, fingers doing the walking, intent on his sticky patrol.

'About what?' I demanded.

Joe looked up. 'About you sleeping in, my friend,' he smiled, innocently – as if. 'What else?'

'Yea, right!' I muttered, guilt stricken. Did he know I had been screwing my sisters? All three of them, bejesus. God I was an animal.

'He goes after the treasure of the *tzitzimime*.'

'Pterodactyl, don't you mean?' I said dully, wondering how I failed to recognise my sisters from the start.

'No.' Joe shook his head emphatically. '*Es* not the same, my friend. The *tzitzimime es. Pterodáctilo está extincto*.'

'And that is the difference?' I asked, grateful for the conversation and distraction from black thoughts.

'Yes!' Joe said emphatically.

'And this, uh, so-called *tzitzimime* treasure – was there ever one?'

'Sure, my friend,' Joe smiled beguilingly. 'Just like you have over there,' he inclined his head at the hotel.

I frowned. 'How many treasures?'

'Thirteen,' Joe said evenly, 'Is the number most sacred to the ancient Tolucans. *El número del sol y del oro!*'

'And the town?' I ventured, reminded of the wayward cathedral clock.

'Oh yes,' Joe nodded, 'We still follow the same system, thirteen hours in the day, and thirteen hours at night, just like the Aztecs have. If you look hard enough, always that lucky number turning up.' He glanced sideways. 'There, you see, in the sugar bowl, thirteen flies. Like the founding fathers of the town, thirteen *conquistadorés* after they find the mother lode, crawling on top of each other to get at *el oro*. Maybe *es* their spirits still trapped here, what do you think?'

Thirteen flies – Castillian knights in shiny armour, getting down to it, mining the mother lode. Yea sure, Joe. Pull the other one-armed bandit, mate. How many treasures? I'd gotten the gist of one already. Mark that down to HRH Hapsburg. So that left twelve, fool's gold, I supposed, camouflage for whatever was real. That longed-for payload? Just dirt, I guessed, unless you scored with Mictlán-te-cuh-tli, as I patently hadn't with my pathetic six intimations. Time for getting back to the hotel and facing up to whatever 'Mother' had planned. Probably my demise I thought gloomily. But wasn't I forgetting someone?

Father! Imminent and transcendent, wherever I looked, guarding the gate to the sun ... Well, in the dusty corner by the stove actually – a beat-up corpse, revivifying, smoking mirrors blinking in time, focusing my way, snuffing my smell. How could that be? And yet there he was, boots clattering cinder-blackened boards, jerking upright, loping purposely towards me. Scary? I'll say, as if this was a messenger from the Lord of Death, stooping to lay a bony hand on my shoulder.

Surely I was getting confused, for the corpse of my poor father was that old retainer on sentry duty, in the lobby of the hotel. Before me was merely the latest manifestation of my projected need for a father figure. Whether chained in a chest and buried under the flagstones of my room, suited in armour in the hotel lobby or this half-dead vagrant, grinning vacantly – what was the difference really? He was only a lonely old *caballero* in need of company, just as I was.

6

THE LONG MARCH

Hours since we set off. *¿De dondé eres?* This dusty *caballero* my guide, left behind by Jaime apparently – as Joe had explained – hiding out with the mountain 'injuns', somewhere beyond the dawn. Not even dusk yet and already the temperature was plunging below zero, our hoary breaths spaced behind like stepping stones suspended in the still air, the pale sun dipping towards a saw-tooth skyline marching with snow-dusted peaks, this *burro* trail winding up the witchy mountain, swallowed in shadow, resonating to jitterbug hooves. Ahead, the Grim Reaper, bent backed over his big black mule, swaying in his saddle, leading the way. Father? Not exactly, but somehow. Just an old *gringo* panhandler, the last of his kind, living so long with the mountain injuns the cat had got his tongue, according to Joe.

A cat? More like a cougar, I considered, the old-timer responding to a distant howl echoing the canyons, standing stick steady on Spanish silver stirrups, cupping mittened hands to his mouth, chilling my blood with his animal rendition. A coyote, I guessed. So he was not entirely mute. Man-coyote, then. But which half was human? The beastly half, I guessed, thinking of the society left behind. My nymphomaniac half sisters. Helga and her consuming lust. The gold that makes men mad. For why? Perhaps we were all aliens, prisoners of our own device, our much vaunted humanness just concealment from the awful truth that there is nothing beyond the stars but ourselves. The immortals, hiding out from eternity, blinkered in miserable lives.

Introspection, always a dangerous tendency – never more than then, my mule lurching, beneath me pebbles scattering over an abyss. Just concentrate on the *now*. That distant glittering, a chance reflection on mica? But no, there was movement between fishtailing mountains gone scaly with mist. A *burro* train – donkeys and natives shouldering packs – a white man bearing his burden, leading the way, his burnished pate gleaming gold in a shaft of sunlight, penetrating the haze. That had to be the Baron on his quest for *tzitzimime* treasure. Just as well he was headed in another direction, I thought, regarding cloud curtains closing in, sealing a Hapsburg's fate. For glory or bust? Bust, I guessed. Pushed from behind, dashed over rocks, a pterodactyl feasting on his brains. Perhaps that's what he really wanted. Expurgation of ancestor guilt and union with a living fossil. A dinosaur just like himself.

7

BEING TAILED

Premature night as we rode into a dark defile. Basalt outcrops, and icicle fangs welcoming us with the engaging smile of a shark. Or perhaps that was an effect of peyote. Whatever. Plenty more buttons in my pocket to keep me awake. God didn't I need them, I was so tired. Entering the picture, another black-backed hunter, announced by thunder rolling over razor ridges – only those were rotors not fins, cyborgs in beetle armour, behind the bubble eye. The Mexican Army scouring the mountains for what? Bandits or pterodactyls? Or bandits mounted on pterodactyls? That sure would pose a threat to the northern nation. A new superhero, to outflank stealth bombers. They wouldn't be interested in a couple of *sombreros* on mules. Or would they? I was certain of nothing, I might even be hallucinating all this, off my head on peyote, safe in my bed back in the hotel, wishing to god I was wrapped in blankets instead of a coarse woollen serape, one or more of the Malinchés nibbling my toes. That would explain the awful numbness, the untoward pelvic throbbing, this strange disembodied feeling that half of me was looking down on the other half – wondering what the hell I was doing, entering Gehenna, first circle of hell, damned if you do and damned if you don't, flaming mists fired by the

33

rolling red ball of the setting sun, below us as we crested the last ridge.

A fanfare of trumpets wouldn't have been amiss, I thought, gratefully laying my head on steaming flanks.

'There, you see!' That biltong voice, an extension of an old-timer's grizzled mien – all cracked and crusty, just as I would have imagined. Yes, and real. *No peyote hallucination this.*

'Look!' He pointed beyond the sun, dipping towards a fissured caldera crowded by three icy peaks, marching with us through our pilgrimage, only now the eminences were cloaked in royal purple, like a conclave of cardinals. 'That's where we're headed, son, *los dédalo del diablo*, the devil's labyrinth,' he chuckled.

'Fuck!' I cursed, rubbing saddle-sore joints. 'Why talk now and not before?'

'Because I'm dead back there, son,' he said, drawing deep on oxygen thin air. 'Only here am I really alive. Comes from living *alto* so long, I guess.'

Twisting round in his saddle, he grinned lopsidedly, his deep-set eyes glittering in magenta sockets, as he faced me. 'The name's Coyote, son. It's a real privilege to help any friend of Jaime's.'

'So you *do* know him!'

'Of course, son. He is our hope.'

'What do you mean, *hope?*' I said, shivering, my euphoria of a moment before sinking with the setting sun.

'Plenty time later, son,' he said, gathering slack reigns in a mittened hand. 'Still a long way to go.' Turning, he pointed towards a track leading down through the rocks. 'That's our trail.'

'What?' I exclaimed, alarmed by this new development. 'It's almost dark already. We have to find shelter now, surely?'

'No,' he shook his head. 'Full moon on the rise.' He thumbed back the way we had come. 'Soon be bright enough to read a book, if you were that way inclined. Perfect conditions for a trek, son,' he chuckled.

'Yea, sure, Pops,' I muttered, maintaining my fantasy of hanging out with the dad I had never known. 'Whatever you say.'

Nothing else to do but follow my guide between hungry boulders, monuments marking the march of time and hapless travellers turned to stone, their features distended by the prevailing wind, whipping up as we rode on, numb to our saddles. Perfect conditions, huh. And this a mere trek, I considered dismally. Alright for him, 'ornery old mountain goat, in his leathery armour of hide and buckskins, acclimatised all these years. I had to take peyote just to keep up, never mind hold off the toothache brought on by altitude. This was alien turf to me. Except there wasn't any turf, just pockets of snow concealing chasms and worse between the boulders. Suddenly, a masked bandit on a scythe, slalomed on a scythe out from between the humped shapes of the petrified army encamped around, and in a puff of snow, took off, soaring on his scythe over the pink disc of the full moon rising at our backs as, below, an alien army gave voice in a chorus of cracking sounds echoing the fissured glacier. Ghostly faces animating, leering with ghastly grimaces, offering skeletal embraces, like this was a dance of death, and ahead that really was the Reaper, waving his sickle, leading me down, down into his kingdom of night. Another intimation, a gilt edged RSVP, from the Lord of Death, impossible to refuse. Dark fires burning down there, as if the sun was journeying into an infinity of ice. An illusion, I reasoned, just a glacier reflecting the stratospheric clouds turning blood red in the glimmering dusk.

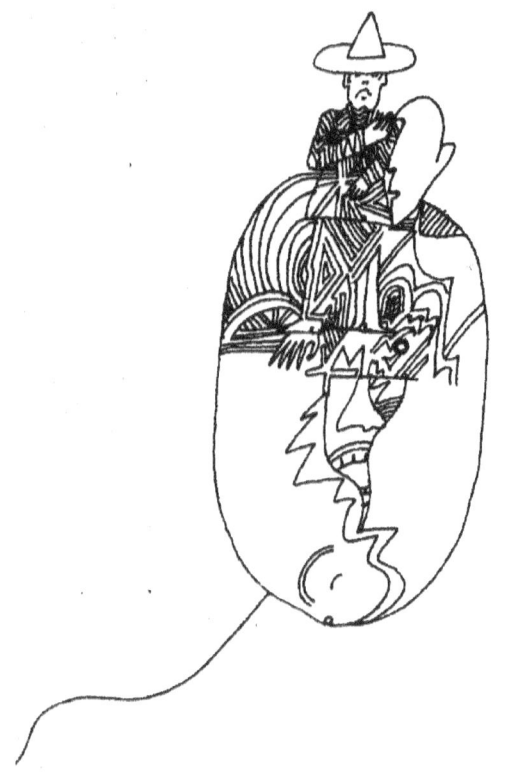

8

THE LOBOTOMY KID

Why ride when you can walk? Why indeed? A point of honour, my guide explained, our mules noble beasts deserving the last of our rations and, besides, both were exhausted. Etiquette of the mountains, or a test? I settled for the second possibility, trying to keep up. Meanwhile my mentor in trackless white wastes turning garrulous, the nearest corner of his mouth working overtime, keeping up a constant repartee. Well, he tried. Maybe he thought I needed distracting.

It seemed he'd come to the mountains to get away from the 'lectricity'.

'Come again?'

'Power lines, son. Can't abide 'em. Make ma brain fizz; what's left of it anyhow. Lobotomised y'know, they took the best part, leavin' me like Ah'm now, more dead than alive. Scraps for the thunder birds if the injuns hadn't gotten to me first.' He pulled back on the reigns and, stopping his mount for a moment, lifted his *sombrero*, revealing a circular scar on his temple.

'Who's they?' I managed, shouting into the wind.

'They'm,' he insisted, 'Southern 'lectric Power, if you believe in a name. The shit-eaters took me down to the third circle of hell, below Uncle Mo's office in Galveston. Didn't matter Ah was family, not when I knew what I knew and was prepared to use it.' He pointed to his head. 'Ah still got the big picture, but Ah forgot all the detail, an', as every critter knows, the devil's always in that.' He spat. 'But that didn't stop them setting the *cousins* on ma tail, comin' in the middle of the night, whenever I got nice an' cosy with a *muchacha*, burning down more'n half a dozen shacks, men in black hounding me all the way through Texas into Mexico, 'till Ah lost 'em in these mountains. Thirty years ago, that was.'

'But why, for god's sake?'

'Punishment for leaking information 'bout the net they aimed to wrap around the world, just as the Spooky Tribe said they'm would.'

'Mobile phones?' I said, remembering a Hopi Indian prophesy about a net that would bring about the end of the world.

'Yea, that's one of the details. Of course, it's disaster for the bees.'

'How?'

'Ah forgot.' He tapped the scar on his head. 'Something to do with base stations complicating bee signals, ah seem to recall. 'Course, when bees stops pollinating, crops don't grow and everyone starves. But a smart fellow like you knows that.'

'Anything else coming through, Pops?'

'Nope.' He shook his head. 'I'm disconnected. Like Ah said, lobotomised since I was hardly more than a kid. Ask again in a few minutes, son.'

'I will, Pops. If you didn't know more, I guess they wouldn't have harassed you all those years as they did. There's no profit in it.'

'Tell that to the cat that plays with the mouse. They'm wouldn't let me live, but wouldn't let me die, neither.' He sighed. 'That's the way it was in the company before they closed the circles. It's worse now that fortunes five hundred's running the show, even the mightiest nation on earth don't matter a darned thing. The good ol' USA, home of the brave an' free, takin' orders from they'm shit-eaters jest like the rest. They weren't goin' to let a squirt ruin their plans, blabbin' to hippie journals, or anythin' like that.' He paused, looking at me strangely, which for him was strange indeed.

'Ah remember now,' he continued, absently picking at ice pocketing his cavernous cheeks. ''lectricity don't need wires and such like to get about. It's freely available, under our feet. The earth, spinnin' on the galactic turntable, a nine-track planet, symmetrically repeatin' orbital shells, tectonic plates in internal gridlock, with a wormhole bang in the centre. A point of collapsed matter, as small as small can be, accordin' to Uncle Mo,' he snorted disdainfully. 'But in mass, no more nor less than all they'm circles above, pumpin' out the buildin' blocks of onion- skin reality, photons an' 'lectrons, jest like the black heart of the sun only nearer. It's how to tap into it, that's what they don't want you to know. So they wired up this world, corrallin' every city, upsettin' the earth's nat'ral power lines, targetin' sensitives, siting transformers an' pylons an' God knows what else, right next to schools and anywhere ordinary folks hang out, wrappin' whole communities in bad vibrations jest so no one cottons on.' He chuckled dryly. 'If they ever do, the cancer economy's finished. Free!' he spat. 'Corporations jest can't handle that word, cuts the market right from under them. That's why they hates the little Mexican injun so. In these mountains, corn is king, not dollars. The peso's useless thanks to all Uncle Sam's done, greenbacks only good for buying *gringo* guns and cars. Co-operation, that's how folk's gets on. Competition! All that's good for is runnin' rats in mazes.'

41

9

FAR PLANET

Famingo dawn, or just under-lighted *tzitzimime* wings overhead, I couldn't tell, back in the saddle, high on altitude and *mezcal* from the gourd my guide occasionally passed over, which was just as well because I was down to my last two peyote buttons. 'Unpleasant' was not adequate to describe the weather beyond the down-turned brim of my *sombrero*, the ranging wind bringing fresh flurries of snow with every gust.

Yes, but why the ominous rumbles always preceding rampaging cracks and accompanying detonations, and the distant plumes spied over a crystal landscape? According to my companion, the natives called this cloudy region the Well of the Worlds. There was even a crater, created by asteroid impact in the remote geological past. Under these unmapped mountains, he insisted, concealed from satellites by the glacier, was the greatest confluence of subterranean rivers – transcontinental amazons down there, some even navigable – the seven tenths of rainfall not run off the surface that has to go somewhere, wearing through the hardest rock. I'd have had to be mad not to believe him, after all he was my guide.

Los dedaldo del diablo, there it was, the devil's labyrinth, a fissured caldera of red entrails garnishing a crusty pizza base in a take-away of *chilé* canyons, packed tighter than the maze at Hampton Court Palace. A multiple-choice scenario obviously, with the added bonus of ice-rimed boulders precariously balanced above gloomy defiles.

One old coyote, reverted to muteness, leading the way on his hardy mule, standing on silver stirrups, pointing up at rock overhangs, cautioning the need for silence. As if I needed reminding. After a few turns, the windswept snow gave way to drifting red sand, banked around large fallen stones, one boulder so big it almost blocked the narrow canyon, adding to the omnipresent sense of danger. Easy to defend this place, I thought, a few braves concealed behind the boulders looming the cliff tops could hold back the Mexican Army.

Then, at one branching of the canyons, old Coyote seemed to lose his bearings, but, after dismounting, on hands and knees he felt along the cliff base until his fingers found what he was looking for – an ancient petroglyph of a feather pointing the way.

Wood smoke, acrid and welcome, indicating there *was* human life hereabouts. Coyote grinning back, his two remaining front teeth very white in the half-light, as if he was a phantom Indian guide, and we both had died. Maybe we had? Tiredness washing over me in waves; hanging in there by the pommel of my Spanish saddle. My exhaustion all but dispelled, however, when, rounding the next bend, we entered a half-moon canyon, the facing rock wall vivid red and deeply fissured. Old Coyote slowing his mule as I drew up alongside. 'D'you see anything particular, son?' he asked, at last breaking his rule of silence.

'Can't say I do, Pops,' I croaked, my throat dry.

'Look harder, son,' Coyote insisted, pointing out the striations of weatherworn cliffs, which, as I peered, became monumental Indian braves, close packed as teeth. No way was that the work of wind and rain. All of a sudden something flashed within a cleft. There was life beyond this canyon, I realised, that crack in fact a gap. We were almost home, a big word in that high country. Like finding a habitable planet in the vastness of space. All but impossible without a phantom *gringo* guide. That last thought, confirmed when I looked around – Coyote and his mule were nowhere to be seen. And no tracks neither. The only life about, one 'ornery old fly in shiny armour, weaving pieces of eight around my eyes. Nothing else to do but venture on, with questions in my mind and no father on hand to answer them. One of these days I would admit it – the world was my father – and leave it at that.

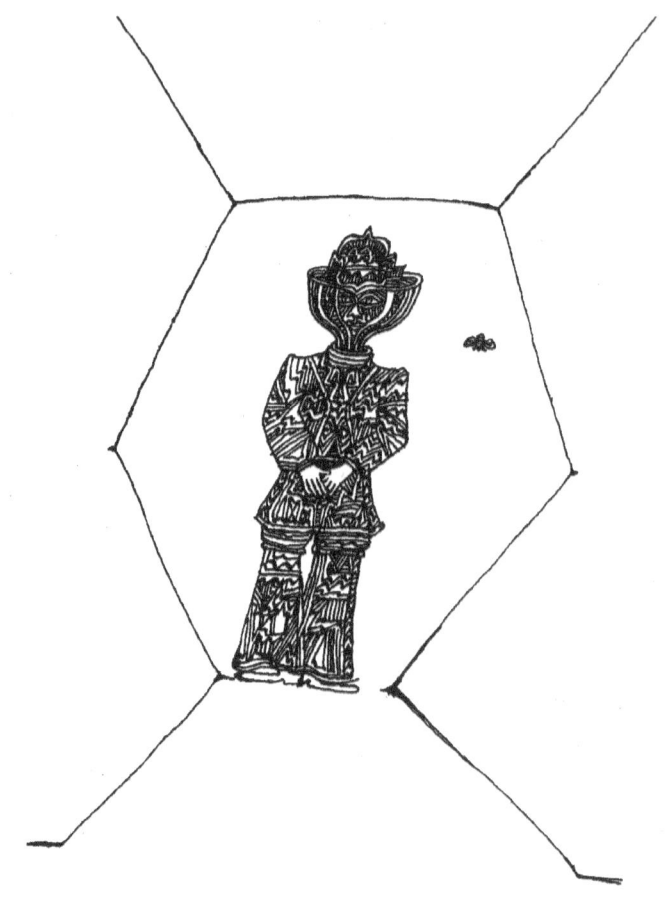

9

THE BEE KEEPER

'Jaime!' I gasped, looking up as I crawled a narrow passageway, its red stone smoothed by the touch of many hands, seeing him at the end, silhouetted by the ascendant sun.

Jaime must have known I was coming, for he was holding out a spliff. Weary after the midnight crossing of the *cordilleras*, the last thing I needed was an enervating smoke.

'Take it!' Jaime insisted. 'Leave that *pinché* fok on the other side. Everyone who enters Happy Valley through that hole is reborn, my *generalísimo*. Take it, is the best my *sapatistas* grow yet!'

I was beginning to make sense of my surroundings. Encircling cliffs, slow- tumbling tertiary time, rock bleached by stratospheric sunlight, fissures and gullies acid scored, magenta shadowed where lower cliffs were buttressed by magma up-crops, etched in ultra violet as I took my second toke. More colour changes as I downshifted, perceiving verdant stone-walled terraces, descending to emerald depths, where water sparkled amid stands of spindly trees. But I was more interested in what was growing in those stepped terraces, looping the flanks of the crater like fingerprints at the scene of a crime. Yes, I knew that shade of green, and I could smell it too, as a light updraft of humid air wafted the unmistakable odour my way. A redolent combination of BO and gruyere cheese matured in dirty socks. Sinsemilla, even at that distance, unmistakable.

Three tokes was all I managed. My *machismo* in question as knees buckled. My, that was superior gage. The best, Jaime had said. I wasn't in a position to demur, swaying metronomically, fighting a geyser rush of polyploids and cannabinoids to my confused but ecstatic brain.

'We grow it for export to Euroland. This year they have the best foking summer since '67. Peace and love in every neighbourhood. We think they need it even more than the *gringos*,' Jaime confided proudly, as we reached the topmost of the terraces spied from above. Bearded, sappy heads brushing my cheeks as we passed through the plantation. The heady scents of best bud only adding to my delirium as I sensed the animating force at the root of all growing things. I could even see it hazily – a magenta, electric aura, pulsing hairy stems. These plants were alive, haloed in energy fields. Despite the light breeze, precipitated pollen hanging over the bushes like clouds of unknowing.

The overgrown trail descended into a series of banked terraces before we came to a clearing filled with a melodic background hum, which I took to be an internal effect of the grass. But then Jaime proudly pointed out a line of conical beehives, buzzing with lazy activity. Workers in syncopated rhythm, communing in the sun, coming and going to the colonies.

'Bee heaven,' he said succinctly. 'Nectar to die for, *generalísimo!*' I was having trouble with the conversation. Everything Jaime said prompted a fit of the giggles, waves of laughter doubling me over, making walking difficult.

'Yea, sure, Jaime,' I guffawed, my jaws aching. 'Next you'll be telling me even the bees give you a buzz.'

'*Es* true, *generalísimo*,' Jaime said indignantly. 'For each harvest fiesta we deep fry and dip in chocolate just as the Aztecs cook them. You never taste the foking like!' 'I believe you,' I said placatingly, my attention distracted by sudden movement at the edge of the clearing. We were under observation, I realised with a jolt, glimpsing ghostly features and long silver hair before the watcher's pale face was concealed by the lowered brim of a scrappy straw *sombrero* as he resumed his task, steadily pruning sappy flowering heads from stout branches, a steady cascade

dropping into a sack tied to his waistband. 'So it's true,' I breathed.

'What you say, *generalísimo?*' Jaime said, giving the native a lazy wave as we followed the path into more dense greenery.

'That was a Christos, right?' I rasped, my mouth dry. 'I'd assumed the albino tribe was just another Mexican tall story?'

'You have it wrong, *generalísimo!*' Jaime chuckled. 'The story of a white tribe and the *Chicano* Jesus crucified by the *Españolos* is a rumour we put out to fool the *satanistas* at the cathedral. That *hombre* is *compañero* Manfred, the foking *número uno* expert on permaculture. He brings a team from the Netherlands to learn us the ways of our Aztec ancestors, who give to the world.' He waved at the lower plantations, lush with variegated colours. 'Chocolate, chilli, corn, tomatoes, peppers, squash,' he grinned proudly. 'With his help, now we get five crops a season.'

'That's just great, Jaime.' I gasped, stumbling on something brown snaking the undergrowth, 'I hope that's water?' I said, relieved the plastic pipe was not the dozing python I first took it to be.

'The purest you ever drink. But foking cold. We have to let it sit in the pipe warming all morning in the sun, otherwise it chills the roots. Glacier floodwater we pump from down there,' he said, pointing at a group of huts, the long roofs shiny with solar photovoltaic cells in a tree-lined ravine where white water frothed in shady depths below red canyon walls. 'The *loco* Dutchmen like to skinny dip in whirlpools there, but is foking dangerous. Only the other week we lose one, so stoned he is laughing as he goes, swept into the tunnels, to where no one knows.'

'Way to go!' I giggled, imagining a laughing Dutchman bobbing away on a subterranean tide. 'At least he went happy.'

'Is no joke,' Jaime said, squaring his shoulders, hands to his sides, huffing like a bar-coded quetzal. 'He is a *Sappatista*, a true hero *de la revolućion*,' he proclaimed, a ridiculous bird, reciting the valedictory. 'We honour his memory.'

'Revolution! Come off it,' I laughed, confident enough to risk the dialectic. 'All this is just business. *Narco*, admittedly, and while the hazards are high, the profits more than compensate. Stay in the game, play your cards right and one day this will all be legal and you'll be head honcho of a zillion-dollar corporation living in a glass mansion in the sun, instead of hiding out here in Happy Valley.'

'For the *pinché* NSA the shit that finances their black operations is legal already. But even you, *generalísimo*, can never call that crap grass, adulterated with foking toxic additives designed to bring on heart attacks, strokes and Alzheimer's in later life.' He bunched a fist, reminding me of an equestrian statue of Bolivar I saw in Caracas, once. 'Quality organic bud like this makes you laugh so much you see through the curtain of lies. That is what the shit-eaters most fear.'

He was interrupted by a sudden roaring, downdraft from above, bending and breaking budding branches all around us.

'Ayee!' Jamie cried into the wind, reaching to his waistband for his pearl handled revolver, yelling to make himself heard over the din, 'Is the foking black thunder birds! Now we die!'

Black thunderbirds indeed. Next he would be telling me we were under attack by the *tzitzimime*. For all I knew, we were. A nightmare feeling of unreality, as we stood shoulder to shoulder, shocked by so many black-backed hunters, blocking out the blue. For Jaime this was the end, and he was determined on a hero's death, but not for me. I was his *generalisimo*, and *generalisimos* - as he reminded me, pushing me protesting into wooded depths where slender white oaks competed for the light - are supposed to lead from the back, live to fight another day. There would be future battles, and delicate flowers of Xochipilli, such as myself, should never engage in the hand-to-hand stuff. Bidding me adieu, he was so sweet, wrapping me in a warm but all-too-brief embrace, by where white water foamed into a dark cavern. Before he turned away, heading up between the tall spindly trees towards a battle zone. Over the next ridge a creeping barrage of incendiaries and shell bursts back-lighting a bristling colossus massing over dense foliage - the deranged genii- loci of Happy Valley - billions of berserk bees rising towards combat-ready cyborgs dropping hand-lines, trailing a fleet of helicopters.

One disquieting sight, unmistakable through tinted Plexiglas, Herr Hapsburg behind the cyborg pilot, strapping on armaments as he prepared for the big drop. Yea, I should have known, his expedition had all along been a ploy, and the shit- eater was a NSA operative, using the hotel as a forward base in a battle plan to seize of the last redoubt of revolution in the *cordilleras*, and take control of this shifting Mexican reality, when aces are low and spades count as hearts, and kings double as knaves.

11

FEAR OF PERSONAL SURVIVAL

Lost, I was lost in echoing passages, resounding with the percussions of distant explosions. The oppressive darkness, relieved only by stray shafts of light, penetrating voids in the rock above. Small stones and dust scattering about my head, cracks opening up in the walls as I ran, trusting more to luck than judgement. Narrowing confines forcing me ever closer to white-water rapids, throwing spray in my face as I stumbled over wet boulders.

A massacre was going on in Happy Valley, and all I had in my favour was a head start. Soon the battle would be over, then, when the baron discovered I was not among the dead, he would come the pursuit.

They were professionals, armed and presumably equipped the latest in tracking technology which would include night sight. My only chance was to put as much distance between myself and the hunters; I was a witness and couldn't be allowed to live.

Faced with branching passages I was undecided. Ahead, the rapids divided around a rocky pier, parting the raging waters before a dark curtain – no light beyond, just the roar of monstrous falls somewhere further on. I had little doubt this was the Well of the World the old *gringo* had spoken of. The two passages, just ahead, both sucking enigmas in a great skull socketed by blackness and my unruly fears. Some *generalísimo*, me. If only Jaime could see me now, I thought, shivering, though not from the cold. Before me that torrent surging up the tunnel walls to either side of the rock pier, leaving no room for passage on foot; I was boxed in, unable to go forwards or back. And now, to add to my terrors, the passage was echoing with the sounds of my pursuers. Lights too, torch beams sectioning the overhead rock in wavering slices. The odd shapes of the leading silhouetted figures, suggested the advance party were cyborgs. Was that a hallucination? But what did that matter, when I was foredoomed. Perhaps I was already dead. There again, maybe not, I thought, making out a faint green glow emanating from behind the pillar.

That eldritch glow reminded me of another light, seen years before it seemed, but in reality only three days previously, when I received the second of my intimations from Lord Mictlántecuhtli. This, then, was my third intimation, his death light showing me the way. But did I have resolution enough to take the plunge? I was out of time, as now the crisscrossing torch beams converged on the rocks where I crouched. It was do and die and the devil take the foremost. Yea, me, I thought, as my head cleaved black waters.

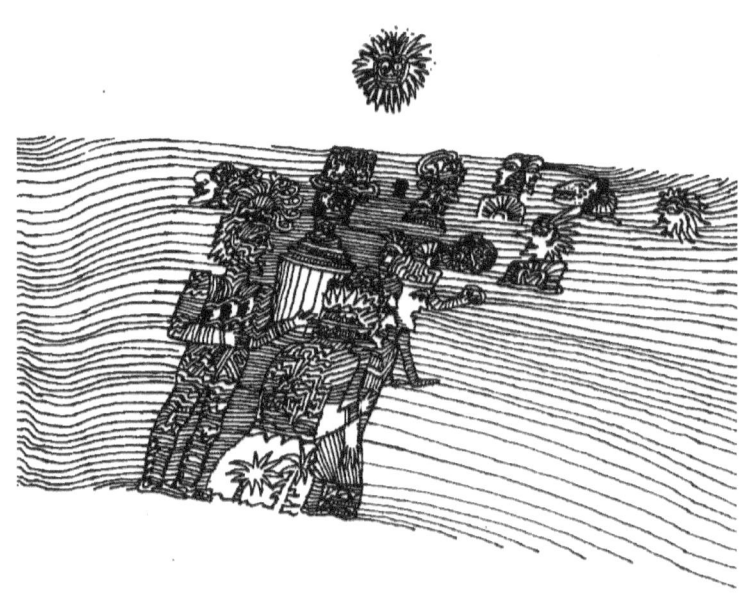

12

SINK OR SWIM, IT'S ALL THE SAME IN THE BLACK RIVER ...

I was a spinning target in a maelstrom, the red flares of bullets zipping past, each time I came up for breath, buoyed by bubbles and the feeling I was not alone, as I swam against the current, praying that my running dive carried enough momentum to take me to the far side of the pillar. Then, as, the basalt pier loomed, it reshaped into a bristling colossus. Fuck me, that was no hallucination. The cracked jig saw of the stone column, anthropomorphising into the standing figure of Archeron, gate-keeper of Hades, bestriding breaking waters, where white spume slicked black rocks. His immense shins an arm's stretch away now, a surge of melt- water taking me round. Nothing to grab, blind luck and the suck of the undertow taking me just under the viscous prongs of a metal sluice, where the vastly bloated corpse of the laughing Dutchman was caught, his bulging eyes staring sightlessly ahead, one forearm trailing the rushing waters, his fingers brushing my head from the cross bar of the sluice just above, pinging with a final flurry of bullets as I was swept on.

On the far side, the crosscurrents seemed to cancel out, leaving the surface glassy with inky turbulences, enabling me to strike out for a stone quay, fifty feet off to the right, and a bronze ring hanging from a monstrous stone mouth that, in the stygian gloom, seemed more that of a living beast, as, with a last desperate effort, I flailed a hand, knowing my fingers were too frozen to hold on, and pushed my arm through the ring. Hanging on by the crook of an elbow, staring at those heavy jowls, I realised I had seen the same stone lions on the embankments of the ports of great cities – London, to name but one – making me wonder if I'd drowned in the crossing and been translated to the far shore of the River Styx.

Somehow I hauled myself up and over that enigmatic pier. Lying with water draining from my sodden clothes, my head resting on cold stone that vibrated with the thunder of the distant falls, I felt warm blood trickling a graze on my shoulder and I was grateful. That and the chill in my bones confirming what I most needed to know. I was alive. But where, and for how long, were questions to which there were no answers, at least not for now. I was entombed more surely than if sealed in a sarcophagus. The weights of the rock above and the crepuscular death light of my demon lord oppressed me with the all-pervasive sense of being walled-up in a mortuary temple. A supposition that seemed corroborated, when at last raising my head, there on the pavement before me, in a clear plastic envelope was a sheet of yellow parchment. A certificate, I saw, blinking blearily. Diogenes was included along with a string of other names, some of which I recognised, others not, under the headline, 'Death Certificate', above an embossed seal of a grinning skull, ringed by the familiar inscription, '*memento mori*', and below that the words, 'Do not hinder or obstruct the bearer'.

So it was confirmed. I had arrived on the far side of the Black River in Lord Mictlántecuhtli's shady realm. Still alive, somehow in corporeal form, yet numbered among the dead, with a certificate that was also a permit to prove it – suggesting in this shady realm I had a privileged status. Unlike those swaddled bundles, occupying countless regular-sized niches in the wall before me, which I knew could only to be row upon row of ancient mummies.

A multitude of the dead that seemed to have no end. For even in this dim, crepuscular, green light I could make out that the wall of niches continued much farther than around the next corner. The broad causeway of the embankment, curving off into the distance, crenulated at intervals where elegant stone bridges, that would have graced a Doge's palace, spanned what I guessed were run-offs for more glacier melt-water – a network of deep channels that, with their architectural grace and style, oddly reminded me of the canals of Venice. Giving me, I supposed, more choice as to direction. Which was just as well, for around that next corner the causeway was blocked by an impassable pile of irregularly shaped stones of smoky grey obsidian. A rockfall from above, I realised, looking up at a jagged fault between grinding tectonic platelets, extending way into the black heart of the mountain above. The glassy fissure spilling more debris as I stared, a scattering of smaller stones raining down, filling gaps between the piled rocks. Some razor- edged splinters bounced the boulders at the base, stotting the pavement, before finally stopping at my feet.

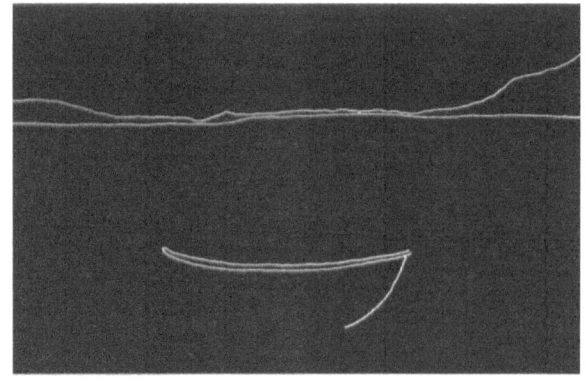

12

THE BOAT

Even before I looked over the dockside, I knew it would be there. The boat, more a skiff really, a long pole laying athwart the gunnels, bumping softly against the embankment wall where wet black steps, spectral in the green light and inset with strange fluorescent fossils, led down to the fast-flowing waters. That it was unmoored and yet stayed where it was should have alerted me to the strange nature of the craft, but I was so keen to secure it, I did not stop on the steps to consider the possible implications.

She was beautiful and slender, with room enough to lie out – why did I think that? I suppose because I already knew. But the knowledge, if indeed I had it, as yet was concealed from my consciousness. Then, as I hauled her broadside on and stepped within curved and caulked cedar planks, I noticed how steady and high she rode in the water. Already, I loved this bonny boat, which was just as well, as I was going to spend some time in her. But that was yet ahead of me. For now, all I knew was that I had a means of navigating this subterranean realm of my Lord Mictlántecuhtli.

'*Speed bonny boat like a bird on the waves, over the sea to Skye* ...'

Unbidden, words of a song from the old country springing to my lips as I punted along, standing balanced in the stern, careful not to stray into the fog bank to my left that obscured the other shore – if there was such – keeping close to the near embankment, for this method of propelling a boat by pole was new to me. One thing I soon observed was the ease with which the craft turned in the waters. Almost as if she anticipated my every move, poling this way and that, following the shore line, negotiating the tricky crosscurrents below narrow arched bridges, connecting regularly spaced wharfs where canals disgorged their contents into the Black River.

So far so good. I even felt cheered. Little did I suspect what was in store, but then all this was new to me and as such I was as an innocent abroad, making the most of exploring drear surroundings. Where even my way of thinking was weird to myself, as if I had taken on an another personality on this far shore, which, though light years from everything I knew, was somehow also deeply familiar, making me wonder whether I had passed through this domain of the dead before. If only the corpse light of Lord Mictlántecuhtli had not been so dim, I would have been able to make out more detail of the cavernous walls towering above the deep canals. A compelling vista reminded me of pictures I had seen of Petra, a lost canyon city beyond the River Jordan, only here the scale was so much greater. Architraves, pillars, ornate entrances hewn into living rock. A compendium of architectural cultural styles – everything from Aztec to Zoroastrian. Classical, Gothic Revival, Fascist, Brutalist and Fin de siècle, and even Post-modern. Every window, doorway, grotto, as far as I could see, vacant except perhaps for further multitudes of mummies stored within. I hoped not, for already the sense of utter oppression, emanating from the endless niches lining the facing wharves, was almost more than I could bear. Little did I know, how much more oppressive they would become in time, which, I didn't need reminding, ground more slowly here than elsewhere.

It was useless to speculate for how long I had been punting when I saw the wandering light. As I have implied, time is ever in abeyance in that shady realm, except when the beacon shines from the left shore. My first sight made me feel that a pointing finger was ripping the very fabric of eternity and piercing the fog bank, before I was caught in its roseate brilliance and, quite unbidden by me, the prow of the boat turned into the beam.

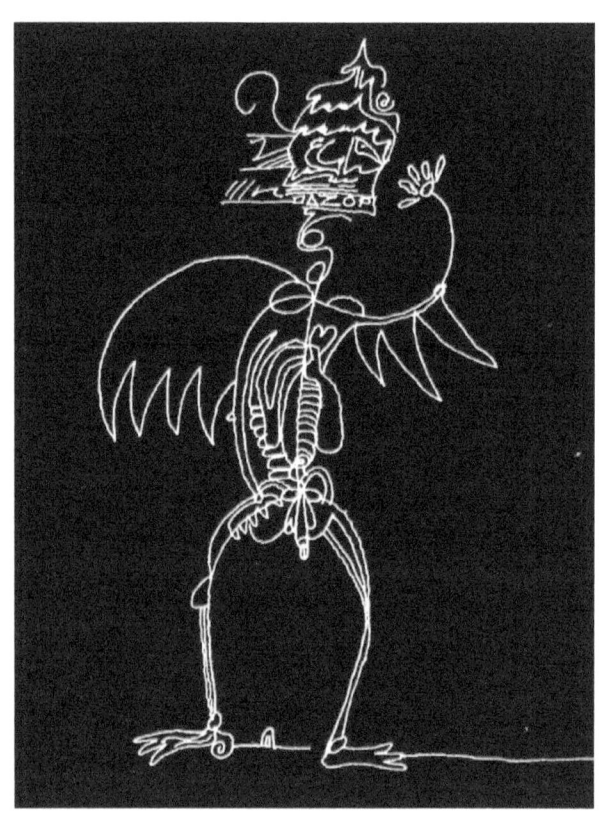

13
BOB THE DEVIL ...

'Don't act stupid, like you don't know,' the foreman said, leaning over the guard rail as, behind him, his saturnine work crew, glowing in their one-piece hooded orange overalls, trundled a covered trailer to the head of the jetty above. 'We've a full complement tonight.'

'Tonight?' I repeated dully, noticing over his shoulder a pale staircase in the distance, ascending cavernous walls towards the yawning entrance of an enormous tunnel, fitfully illuminated by a flickering red light.

'Sorry, mate,' he grinned, revealing a fine set of white gnashers. 'I forget it's always night your side of the Styx.'

'Styx?' I said, appalled to hear confirmation of what I had already suspected. 'Jesus ... fuck!' Next you'll be telling me I'm Charon the ferryman.'

'Too true blue,' the foreman nodded, 'Someone's got to do it. Now can we get a move on?'

'Hold on, I'm new to all this.' I pointed past him to the staircase, where a chain of similarly clad workers were passing down bandaged bundles. 'Where does that tunnel lead to?'

'Gehenna,' he replied succinctly, pushing back his orange hood to wipe away the sweat that trickled his forehead, revealing a neat pair of horns above his temples.

'Never heard of it,' I snapped, struggling to come to terms with what I was seeing.

'The dump of the damned, mate. The penultimate of the nine levels of Mictlán.' Peremptorily he turned, thumbing at the now uncovered trailer, which I saw was overloaded with bundled, bandaged bodies. Some, as I stared, appearing to shift slightly in the trailer, which I put down to settlement brought on by the bumpy ride. 'And those,' he laughed, 'Are the fucking rejects.'

'So who gets to go to heaven?'

'No one.' Shaking his head, he gave me the gladiatorial thumbs down. 'We're all damned.'

'Where's God in all this?'

'There is no God, only Lord Mictlántecuhtli.'

'You sound very sure about that.'

'I am mate. I am.' He grinned. 'Anything else you need to know?'

'Your name will do.'

'Bob,' he said, reaching down, extending a skeletal hand. 'Pleased to meet you, mate.'

A full complement, as my new mate Bob the devil had said, to be individually delivered to the other side before the next load was brought to the jetty tomorrow – whenever that was. At least I was to be compensated. Each of the stiffs came entirely swaddled, except for a gap over their eyes, which were closed by a pair of coins, which, with one notable exception – detailed later – were always 24 carat gold. The dates and countries of the variously named, aureus, bahts, bezants, crowns, cruzados, dollars, dinars, drachmas, ducats, escudos, francs, guineas, guldens, kaulas, kronas, lire, mohurs, obans, pistoles, pounds, pesos, rands, rubles, rupees, sovereigns, talers and other currencies too ancient and worn to decipher, offered no obvious correlation, other than the occasional coincidental correspondences, with either the apparent age or ethnicity of the deceased. Suggesting that the coins were allocated before transit below according to a formula known only by the devils of the relevant upper infernal region, where Bob informed me, judgement took place, before they were sealed in place by wax and set there as payment for the ferryman. Me, evidently.

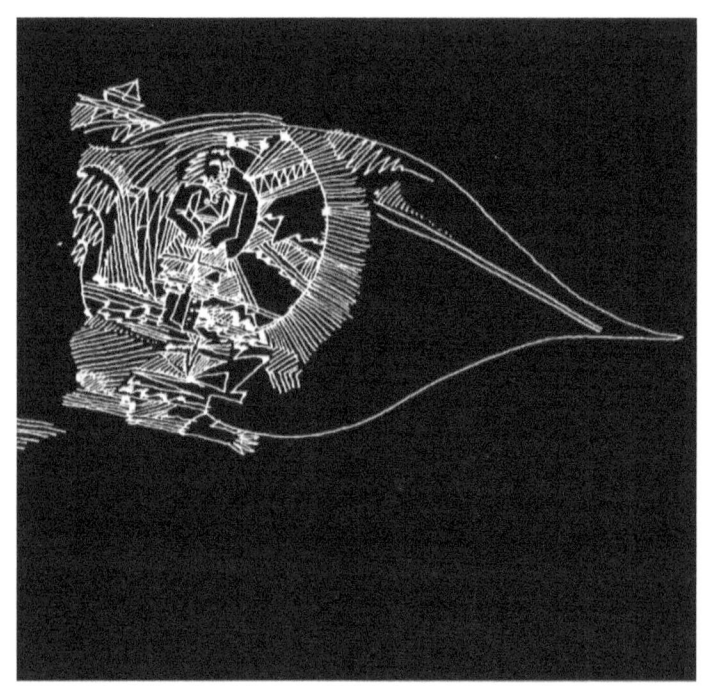

14

JUST A MOTE IN MICTLÁNTECUITLI'S EYE

If only I'd had more room in the boat, I could have taken more. Correction: if only the boat had been willing, I would have taken more. Not the full complement of stiffs certainly, but given the available space, at least three at a time. However, every time I attempted to haul a second body from the lower staging where they had been heaped by the workforce higgledy-piggledy,, the boat lost its characteristic steadiness and began rocking violently, the side-to-side motion threatening to tip the stiff already loaded – and myself – overboard into the fast-flowing waters. Not knowing the ramifications of losing Lord Mictlántecuhtli's precious cargo, and concerned that might mean forgoing his favour in the future, I resisted the impulse, though my urge to rebel against what I regarded as a monstrous imposition was surpassing strong.

At least I was clear as to what my duties were, which is always a help when starting a new job. I also liked the money – rationalising there would be some way to spend it later – though not the means of payment, which initially was distasteful. Even though taking my due, what Bob the devil called the 'ferryman's tokens', made me feel like a tomb robber, guilty of desecrating the dead as I cast the gold coins into the sump of the boat for want of somewhere better to keep my growing collection. But this, I reasoned, was Lord Mictlántecuhtli's realm, and beggars in his employ could not afford to be choosy. Be that as it may, I felt grateful, for it soon became obvious that the mummies I was so laboriously transporting in my little craft were not entirely insensible to their fate. As I manhandled them out of the boat, up the steps, across the causeway and, working my way along the wall of niches, finally shoved them in the next empty slot, little groans and moans told me what I most didn't want to know. Namely that, though catatonic, all were completely conscious of everything going on around them.

'Sleep, little one, sleep,' – a refrain I adopted while about my work. Did it help? Yes, I found it soothed my burden, delivering each to their final resting place on the far shore. Putting the lie to the age-old adage that, in the end, hell is other people.

It was a long time, in relative terms at least, before I learnt how to communicate with them. It might have been years, decades even, who knows? Certainly not Bob, my only friend, who, despite his assured manner, had but a thin grasp of subterranean reality as it was in Mictlán beyond the immediate exigencies of his blinkered existence. Something I learnt that was entirely in keeping with the nature of devils, who, just like middle-management in the higher realms, are task driven, never stray beyond proscribed boundaries and certainly not given to philosophising or indulging in abstract thought. Making them, as conversationalists, on par with drinking chums and casual acquaintances of the kind generally found in pubs and bars, which by then I only vaguely remembered.

But I liked Bob and, in my view, that made him important; not like the stiffs who came and went in ever-increasing numbers, personally delivered into their individual slots to await the end of eternity, when the planet plunges into the sun or is demolished by a giant meteor, which by the nature of things will have to be considerably bigger than the one that tore through the earth's crust and created all these subterranean levels of the damned.

How many levels? I only had Bob's word that there were nine, the first of which was Tláltipec, the surface world, where mortals live in denial of the direction in which they are all bound. For all I knew, there were more levels below, accessed by the Well of the World, into which the spiralling Black River and its many tributaries flowed – including the white-water rapids that had carried me to this far shore. The thundering sound of the falls an ever-present constant with the perhaps inevitable result that, with familiarity, it merged into background noises, just as the blood coursing the veins in the ears, so loud during infancy, recedes throughout childhood until it is heard no more. A slow change, marking the gradual transition into adulthood and decline. A sound that lies forgotten in the mind until dissolution, after which there is time to recall everything in the past, secure and swaddled in linen, separated from one's peers, in the wall that circumnavigates the Well of the World, in the ninth level of Mictlán. And that, just a skim on subterranean reality, below which there are more, many more, hidden depths to plumb.

How do I know this? What makes me so sure? More than anything, because of conversations with the dead, when, fog-bound in my boat, concealed from any watching eyes, out in the middle of the Styx, where thoughts can be shared when two coins are removed and the sealing wax is picked from eye sockets, allowing dusty lids to open. Once they accept their lot, the dead know everything; it's a simple fact. With nothing to gain or lose, all knowledge is open to them. Not that they usually want it. But that's the way of the condition.

The first time I talked with the dead, oddly enough, was with my mother. It was her size that gave her away. The first stiff I'd ever shipped whose head had to be propped up in the prow to accommodate her great length. There she was with the bandages fallen from her face, revealing her dues to the ferryman, the gold coins covering her eyes winking annoyingly in the sepulchral light as I poled the boat into the fog bank. Up 'till then I had waited until safely across the river to unpick the coins, but this time I took my payment when we were but half way. Kneeling in the prow, with my fingernails digging around the milled edges of the coins for the Mexican pieces – twenty pesos, Maximillians as it happened, circa 1866, in unusual mint condition, set in sockets head-side up. Worth an absolute packet, if I ever made it up through Mictlán's shady realms to the surface, where the sun shone gold. That's what I was thinking as her voice spoke clearly in my mind.

'Why do you think of monetary value, when it is your mother you are so roughly handling?'

I was astonished and, perhaps in an attempt to test whether she was still counted among the living, shook her violently by the shoulders.

'That's right, abuse me,' she laughed. 'You could screw me now. That's what you always wanted, isn't it, my dirty little boy?'

I tell you, even in death, she was a combative strumpet, my harpy mother.

Equally disgusted with us both, I left the coins where they were and, retreating to the stern, took up the pole again. I punted with all the energy I could muster, which wasn't much since, in Mictlán, I had to get by without food or sleep.

For the rest of the voyage, no further words were exchanged and, once on the far shore, to my regret, I laid her in a niche without removing those mint- condition Maximillian pesos, which were the best Mexican coins I ever came across in Mictlán. I could have gone back, of course, and asked her all sorts of questions relating to infancy, about my father and what happened after I left the hole in the mountain mining town, but I never did. An uneasy feeling made me suspect, despite her incapacitated condition, that she might get the better of me. Thereafter, I always found some excuse not to look for the niche, the exact whereabouts of which by then, perhaps conveniently, I had forgotten.

15

A DIRTY RASCAL

It was to be a quite a while before anyone else I recognised turned up. How long? A question difficult to answer exactly, as time was a subjective matter in Mictlán. However, by any reckoning, it must certainly have been years. In the meantime there were stiffs too numerous to mention. Conversations too, after adding their dues to my ever-growing pile in the sump and propping them up in the prow. Though I have to admit I soon became choosy, selecting only those with interesting faces or unusual coins. Once I had picked out the coins, how febrile the eyes of my chosen stiffs gleamed in the eldritch gloom, watching me leaning on my pole, punting the last six leagues of their journey, back across the Black River. All were scoundrels of some description or another. Elsewise none would have been relegated to the lowest level of Mictlán, as I had come to believe of the ninth. Included were all the usual suspects, swindlers, grifters, thugs of all kinds – rapists, muggers, murderers, serial killers and worse, I imagine, for not all were open concerning their crimes. But none came near, by degrees of latitude, longitude, turpitude or magnitude to even approaching, let alone matching, the mendacity of the leader who most unwisely claimed that only YHVH, the god of the Hebrews, who, as Jehovah, is also shared by Christians, had the right to judge him. That he'd traduced his country's formerly high reputation and that more wars had been launched on his say so, on mere scribbles on the backs of restaurant menus, than any predecessor had ordered was neither here nor there, as long casualty lists of civilians and combatants were meat and drink to Mictlántecuhtli. Instead, our beholden lord took grave exception to the spurious claim of divine protection according to Bob, who witnessed the judgement – taking a special interest because he knew that the politician in question was already in Lord M's employ.

But those matters did not intrude on our conversation, as much because the salient facts of the politician's rise and fall had faded from my mind, even though previously I was always hungry for the news. No, what concerned me were the experiences we had in common as children, living within a few streets of each other – though my early years were spent in a Georgian rectory, whereas his was a miserable fifties bungalow, a fact which never appeared in his biography – and then boarding at the school I have referred to earlier in my account. Elias Ashmole's. Yes, even in the infernal realm far below the surface level of Tláltipec, the name was burned on my mind, along with its satanic silhouette of three fretted spires that so dominated the north side of that capital city. Yes, we were both old boys, but there were enough years between us to ensure that our paths had never crossed 'till then, staring at each other across the length of a small boat crossing the Black River.

'I know you from somewhere,' I began, by way of initiating conversation.

'I expect that's because I was a player in the great game.'

'Chess?' I frowned, putting him on.

'Global politics, international relations, alliances between super powers, ending poverty – that sort of thing.'

'None of which means anything to me,' I said, ceasing punting and laying the pole athwart the gunnels, letting the boat drift into the descending fog, into the middle of the river.

'I can't believe that. Politics affects everyone's life.'

'Ah, but we're both dead,' I countered, reflexively patting the certificate kept in the breast pocket of my shirt.

'Yes, you're probably right,' his mental image sighed in my mind. 'But I still have my legacy.'

'Indeed, you do,' I grinned. 'Starting with the letters D.I.Y., together with a little symbol suspiciously like a prick with an eye at the tip of the glands.'

'How do you know about that?' he scowled.

'You were a few years ahead of me at school.'

'Elias Ashmole's?'

'Where else could a scholarship boy have picked up such a pukka accent?' I said, reverting to type, if not form.

'So you had a scholarship as well. I got mine on account of my father being an Intelligence officer. What was yours?'

'My father?'

'Yes. Assuming you had one.' He chuckled, feebly.

'He was a Bishop, I seem to recall.'

'My, my. And you the Ferryman. How we've both fallen. Only the right-hand angels, eh? But I still don't understand. D.I.Y. and Diehard Willy were my special secret.'

'Do you always advertise your secrets?'

'Wear them on your shirt sleeves, I say. That way you get noticed.'

'Does that include carving them on the lid of a desk?'

'You really were there, weren't you?' He grinned his famous grin. 'I did that while conjugating Latin verbs.'

'You also did it in the crapper.'

'Yes, I did it lots of times there. And the dorm, and the gym, and the science lab, and home economics. And, after I left, in barristers' chambers when studying the law. Of course there was that famous club in Brussels no one ever mentions ...'

'The shit-eaters?'

'Of course, and I even did it later in the White House when on the pan, though by that time I had no need to leave my mark.'

'Masturbation?'

'Naturally, every public school boy is a wanker. But I took it to a high art.'

'I still don't understand.'

'The bigger the lie, the straighter the face, the greater the thrill. Though the tension of maintaining an even expression does, I find, over a long period of time, strain the muscles of the eye sockets, especially on my left side. At school I had to do it with one hand in my pocket. But through practice, sheer, dogged, bloody minded perseverance, I eventually became so accomplished I developed special muscles in my groin so didn't have to use either hand. I got my rocks off doing TV interviews, answering questions in the House of Commons, at press conferences, giving speeches to Congress, the European Parliament, during Cabinet meetings, banquets and receptions. Everyone knew and yet they couldn't tell. That was my secret of my attraction and the priapic source of my power. The way I cast my spell over millions.'

'And yet you say you had God on your side?'

'I do even now. He sent you, didn't He?'

I had no rejoinder to that and so I broke off eye contact, severing the mind link and shutting the diehard prick in delusory self-gratification forever and forever and forever. Amen.

Yes, just another posturing politician consigned to the

dustbin of history, a reject relegated to the wall of niches in Lord Mictlántecuhtli's shady realm. Oh, and by the by, before I leave the subject, that dirty rascal's fee for the crossing proved worthless; the two coins unpicked from his sockets were not gold as I originally believed and was customary, but gilt through and through – the same as his conscience, I suppose.

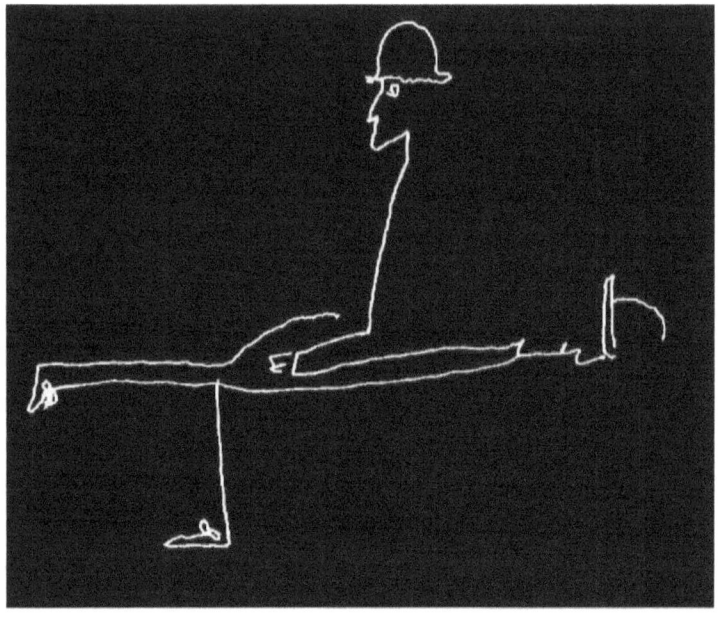

16

TURNED-UP ...

Before I go on, there's something I should explain. In Mictlántecuhtli's realm, I was in a translated state. Just the same as all those stiffs so laboriously transported shore to shore, to their final resting places in the wall of niches. Each bandaged bundle representing the immortal residue that cannot be destroyed, whether by fire, petrifaction or other processes. Of course, by the favour of my guardian demon, I was blessed with more substance, otherwise I could not endured the backbreaking toil, the endless tedium, the lack of sleep and food, the malicious gleam I beheld in the beams of many evil eyes – the price I had to pay for a bit of company and a few shared words, as wearily I poled my cargo across the Black River. Charon's lot was a bad bargain, I tell you, in the matter of Faustian pacts. But it was mine to endure and besides, bit by bit, coin by coin, my pile in the boat's sump was growing steadily. Translated gold, of course – that immortal residue sought by the alchemists, such as the great Paracelsus, otherwise the overloaded boat could not have ridden high in the waters. But gold none the less. All mine, yes, and recompense despite the fact I had nowhere to spend it.

Perhaps I had a fever – gold fever, the same as struck down the conquistadors, a malady from which there is only one relief, as Cortez explained to Moctezuma. Yes, you've got it, more gold. Which, in my case, came two coins at a time.

I was gouging out my next pair, scraping at the sealing wax filling the sockets, when I recognised some familiar features under the parted bandages. Who else, but my father? The prominent brow, praetorian nose and saturnine jowl; unmistakable. Kneeling astride his slumped form, propping his head and shoulders against the prow, I hesitated, unsure whether I could endure a conversation I had so desired for such an inordinate length of time.

My father, just the thought of him was enough to threaten my translated immortal state. Would he reject me all over again? If so, what would I do? Throw myself overboard? But then this was Mictlán, so therefore suicide, and consequently drowning, was not a possibility. I had to take the risk. After all, what did I have to loose, since I was dead anyway? Yea, with a certificate in my shirt pocket to prove it.

'My son! At last I've found you!'

Yes, that's what he said as his eyes blearily focused on my face. I couldn't believe it. Of all the insults in the after world, that took the biscuit. This bastard was gagging on it, and so I did not reply, just staring back at the pupils in his sardonic hooded eyes. Yes, I knew him. That basilisk gaze was written on my mind. An acid stare, received drip by drip, from birth, cradle, through infancy, 'till the artful old dodger skedaddled so prematurely out of my life. Never mind my illegitimate status in a higher realm; he was the bastard.

'I've searched the realms of the dead high and low, and now, approaching the far shore, here you are. By Mictlántecuhtli's beard, it's a miracle.'

'I suppose I have to give you that,' I glowered. 'But couldn't you have found me earlier?'

'I tried, my son. But after the scandal, when I was stripped of my bishop's vestments and exposed as a philanderer in the newspapers, your mother and I separated, and thereafter her lawyer always denied me access. She had been my housekeeper you see.'

'Yes, I know about that. I looked her up in a hotel in a town, you might have heard of it, though it has no name.'

'Of course I know it. And the hotel, which I bought with the profits of several mines I owned in and around.'

'So how did you, a defrocked bishop, end up in the mining business?'

'It's long story, one that started shortly after your birth, when it was discovered I'd sired a son. I was forced to resign holy orders and so my travails began. Now that I've found you at last, that's all over.'

I smiled, thinking of the long search that had finally brought me to the Town With No Name. 'Yea, I can understand that. You might think it's funny, but I even thought I'd found you once.'

'Oh yes?' he beamed. 'And where was that?'

'In the hotel lobby, you might even know it, that mummy encased in conquistador armour. My mother said she bought it from the Black Friars up at the cathedral.'

'She did indeed, but that was no ordinary mummy. It was your forefather, the head of the Inkenhaton clan, an ancient Egyptian plundered from Mictlán by the Black Friars.'

'I don't believe that. We're all ghosts here in Mictlán. You stiffs are just the immortal residue of bodies, many of whom, I am sure, no longer exist in physical form.'

'Ah, but what has been lost in translation can be recovered and even, in some cases, resurrected. Never forget that the surface of the world is but Tláltipec, the first of Mictlántecuitli's nine realms, and populated not by the living, as the ghosts there imagine themselves to be, but by shades like you and me.'

'That's too difficult a concept, even for me, Father.'

'Just accept it, my son. The material body is only a desam manifestation of the self. Don't forget that, here, in this the ninth realm, the immobile dead, "stiffs" as you describe us, know everything.'

'So how the fuck do I get back up to Tláltipec with all this gold?'

'Ah, now you're thinking like a true Inkenhaton, my son,' he said. In that dark place, his smile was like the setting sun, lighting my mind with golden rays.

My father was the last stiff I set into the wall of niches. But not before I resealed his eye sockets with the two gold eagle dollars he'd come arrayed with. Tears of true repentance, spilling my cheeks as, reverently, I stooped to kiss his forehead, begging forgiveness for all the curses and black thoughts I had sent his way. My emotion letting me know I was in transition – no longer a mere shade, but once again possessed of a soul, becoming corporeal, solid, flesh and bone again. Just as well, because his immortal residue was that heavy, I thought I would splinter under the load, bearing my filial burden, heaving him up the embankment steps, across the causeway and, finally, to his last resting place. After doing my duty, I stood for a long time, contemplating his still form, then, before I turned away, reciting a prayer, beginning with these words:

'My father, who art in Mictlán, hallowed be thy name ...'

But then a dream came back on me. My memory of the once-familiar world of Tláltipec returning with a dream of the life I might have had, sharing the same house with my aged father, sometimes hardly speaking for days on end, living like lodgers in the draughty presbytery, leaving our plates and dirty laundry for the only woman in our lonely lives – the cleaning lady whose name I can never remember – sometimes exchanging grunts as we pass on the stairs in the morning, shaving foam still adhering the bristles of his septuagenarian ears, in his red dressing gown briskly making his way down to breakfast, while wearily I ascend to my attic room, after working the late shift at the newspaper where I am employed. Only on Sundays do we eat together, an old family ritual by habit become Sephardic tradition, when we catch up on the news of the week, often talking late into the night. Reminiscing about happy days when the world was young, drawing draughts from the wellsprings of being, where our souls were once joined – when my glass gets empty, he winks and, half grinning, refills it with Arrak, his favourite tipple from his Egyptian days, the drink of sheikhs and common Bedouin, reserved for Sundays and the precious time we share. My father, missing always, but somehow not. Within me and without me, those parts somehow separated by a chasm, unbridgeable, and yet not. Waking into another dream in this life I never had, I sometimes feel such grief at my loss; anger too, like vitriol and water brimming my cup, and someone has just applied a match to my phosphorus brain, incandescent rage, rekindling a brush fire in my memory. My father at the western limits of the world, mourning his loss and mine. His after-image searing into my mind, as he stands back turned before an abyss, arms spread, a winged worm, black against the setting sun.

'My father, who art in Mictlán, hallowed be thy name ...'

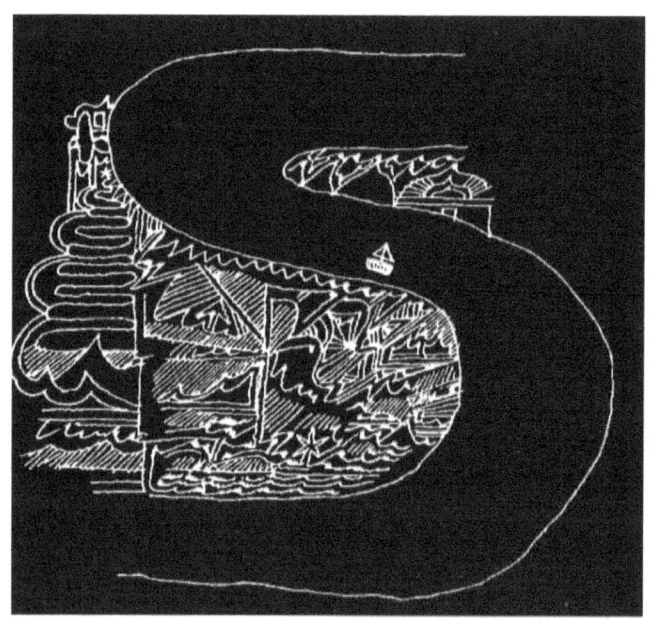

17

SAIL ON

It was the Day of the Dead and, technically, according to the regulations of the establishment, I was entitled to a day off. Trouble was, I needed the cooperation of a small boat. A very stubborn little boat, who *would* keep turning back towards the other shore where, I had little doubt, Bob the devil was already waiting on the jetty with another load of stiffs. But I was within my rights, and stronger now that I was transitioning back to flesh and bone. Moreover, in my Faustian pact with Lord Mictlántecuhtli, I'd never agreed to this posting. A detail, I knew I'd be unwise to mention to the little boat, who was riding lower in the water, suggesting that my cache of gold coins, stuffed in a collection of small sacks, artfully woven from bandages filched from the immobile dead, safe in the sump, was also in transition back to a base state. So, assuming a commanding position, standing in the stern, I produced the plastic envelope from my shirt pocket and, removing the parchment with a flourish, read out what I hoped was now a redundant death certificate, sternly reminding a contrary little boat that, on the express order of the lord of this realm, it was her beholden duty not to 'hinder or obstruct' my wishes, whether or not she approved of the new direction on which I was intent. I did not mention my real purpose for wishing to head upriver, for acquainted as I was with the stubborn nature of the boat, I knew that would have been the end of the matter and the plan hatched after mulling over my father's account of his exploration of the lower reaches of the Black River and the country beyond. The old boy made the most of the interregnum before judgement, searching high and low for the son he had become convinced was also indentured in Mictlán's halls – a supposition that, though premature, ultimately proved to be correct, as it turned out. As the journey wore on, our pace steadily quickened, the current gaining in strength with the torrents out-flowing every passing canal, only adding more water into the Black River. I noted other changes too. Prior to our little jaunt, I'd been confined to working a stretch of the Black River lying within two wharves of the place where the wall of niches terminated in a rough protrusion of rock. This, as I later came to understand, was the last existing uncut section of natural cliff remaining anywhere along the entire length of that left bank, tumbling into the river close to the sluice gates marking my point of entry. Suggesting that in Mictlán everything had its limits, even eternity itself. For, if time wasn't measured by the wall of niches, I couldn't imagine what could be, except perhaps the ultimate span of humanity's tenure on earth. Not something I ever worried overly much about, especially not then, seated in the stern of the speeding boat, with nothing else to do but observe both shores of the river. To my right, regularly spaced jetties along the bank, steps behind leading up to dark tunnel entrances, all marked by a singular lack of activity. No devils anywhere to be seen. With the consequence my attention was drawn more to the opposite shore, where the architectural styles of the edifices lining the boulevards, bisected by canals, were in constant transition. On one street I observed, hoary old statues of Egyptian gods fronting ancient Greek amphitheatres on either side of the canal, while on another, Easter Island heads glowered back, as though across the Pacific, at colonnades of giant figures with scowling Mesoamerican faces. The course of the river itself was changing too, every now and then the surging black waters, were divided by successions of islet promontories into widely separated channels, which merged only after diverging widely through low tunnels, worn through solid rock. But even then there were niches, lining the wall to my left. Every one occupied with a swaddled bundle. At such moments, the multitude of the dead seemed to press in with a claustrophobic, cloying intensity. Our passage was all the more uncomfortable until we re-joined the other branches and Black River broadened out again.

18

FLIGHT ...

What did I say about the current strengthening? No turning back now, for we were caught on the dragnet of the ever-more deafening falls, concealed somewhere behind the drifting veils of spume, rising in billowing, back-lit cloud curtains, outlined by brilliant violet discharges flashing from electrical storms beyond. Coalescing, against the cavernous vault above, into cumulous thunder stacks, towering over the spectral lady of the mist, looming to our right in the middle distance. A natural spur of fluorescent white calcite, jutting the black headland, behind which, according to my father, lay the tributary we had to follow. But in this driving rain, we were shipping water from all angles, waves slopping the port side, forcing me to abandon punting, get down on my knees in the bilge and bail furiously, now utterly reliant on that bonny wee boat to steer a course to safety. The only one in prospect a stretch of calmer water in the lee of the white lady, meaning that the boat was having to tack up, down and back up again through the steeply furrowed foaming black torrents. A parting in the clouds off to the stern revealed the architecture of the falls, flash-lit by a jagged bolt of lightning striking way below. Just a glimpse, but enough to convince me; here were a multitude of black rivers, cascading an infinite-seeming series of cupcake gradations, stepping right down into what looked to be the sphincter of the world. A sucking, puckered, staring, black eye towards which we were surely headed. But no, at the last moment, when it seemed we were doomed to pitch over, the stubborn boat righted herself, turned, the prow dipping and then violently rearing – almost up- ending in the process – and suddenly we were suddenly flying, the keel clearing the crest of the ultimate black roller, before splashing down in the leading finger of that long stretch of calm water.

19

STAR FISH

Incredibly, we were through, and I still had my gold, half-submerged in the sump but safe, payment from a multitudes of stiffs – all but one of whom I wished to forget. The ardour of my time as the ferryman was already fading as, taking up my pole again, I resumed punting, knowing the boat had no other choice but to cooperate and steer a course up the tributary, aiming for a tiny point of white light that, in the darkness, looked just like a twinkling star, suggesting we were voyaging across the heavens, instead Lord Mictlántecuhtli's shady realm.

It seemed I had slept, for I found myself laying on a sandbar, the sacks of gold scattered about me, by a gushing spring – I guessed the source of the tributary. The bonny boat, however, was nowhere to be seen. My first thought was that it had voyaged on to that star, which was still shining strongly in the darkness yonder. Perhaps it had, for there was no sign of it anywhere along the winding tributary behind, in the corpse background glow a prussic-acid smear holding a pale mirror for the vaulting stone above, fading into the crepuscular green gloaming, in the opposite direction to which I was now headed, but this time by foot.

Was it a star? I wondered, fixing my gaze on the distant luminary, imagining, sailors far out to sea in the world, doing the same, comforted by the thought, feeling not quite so alone, then. Feeling my way forward into darkness, the crepuscular light fading with every forward step now I that was leaving Mictlántecuhtli's realm. After a while even the star seemed to dim, though the inky blackness about it appeared to have been replaced with a smudge of indigo blue. Like the sky as it sometimes appears in the twilight before dawn, I rationalised, remembering life before I joined the multitudes of the dead. But that was behind me, or so I fervently prayed, intent on a tiny patch of brightening blue, around which I could discern a shifting of mottled colour, reminding me of something I'd seen long years ago, before I fell into to that shadowy realm below.

20

TEARDROPS FROM TLÁLTIPEC

Left, left and right again – always followed by an immense sucking straight. All I had to do was remember the formula and I couldn't go wrong. But my father obviously had no inkling how life is for dyslexics – how even the simplest directions can overload the brain. Mine was steaming in this clammy subterranean heat. Perhaps I had misheard and it was the other way round? If so, I could have approached the Well of the Worlds the wrong way and be under Africa by now, that deafening roar the Limpopo, or maybe the cataracts of the White Nile disgorging by the Mountains of the Moon – and me with them, if the passage wall to my right gave way.

Maybe I was heading back in a circle, approaching the Well of the Worlds again, that oncoming clamour of lost souls cast overboard by Bob the devil, who I imagined to be the next stand-in ferryman, bumping the bottom, damned, damned and down. Down to Davey Jones' locker, not, as I pre-supposed, at the bottom of the ocean, but in Mexico, guarded by *las tres hermanitas*, concealed under the multiple stratum of voluminous stone petticoats.

Of two things I was sure, I was lost and my father's formula was redundant, with a massive cave-in blocking the ascending passage up ahead. Evidence of the continents cracking up, I supposed, taking a breather, setting down my sacks of gold, which had been growing heavier with each forward step, before scrambling up the baking rubble, intent on investigating whether there was a way through. Only, as I neared the top, the realisation finally dawning that this wasn't a cave-in, but a dump of desiccated body parts. Detritus of mummies, I presumed, plundered from the levels below, confirming what my father said about the Black Friars, suggesting that the cathedral was located somewhere beyond that circular opening in the passage roof directly above my head, through which I could make out another bull's eye in a vaulted ceiling, framing a circular patch of dawn sky, just the right shade of twilight blue, and some furtive streaks of wispy cloud signalling a fine day in prospect. Yes, the ultimate level of Mictlán, opening onto Tláltipec, the surface of the world I had left behind however many years before. Prompting the thought as I climbed that great midden of mummy parts, would anything be the same when I returned? Obviously not, I decided, because I was changed on the inside more than I could have imagined possible. Perhaps that was why, noticing a skull balanced on the summit, out of scale as a pea on the shoulders of a slumbering giant, I impulsively reached for it.

'Where to now, maestro?' I asked the skull, on the palm of my hand. I certainly didn't expect an answer.

'A la luce.'

After all the stiffs I'd manhandled into their personal l niches, I should have been inured to hearing the dead speak, instead of reacting like I did then; losing my footing, all the funny bits in my face as I slid back down the pile scapulae, tibias, humerus, carpalis, patella, metacarpals, tarsals, phalanges, even the dirt seemed composed of bone splinters, bound together by desiccated fibres more fucking shrouds ...

Then, like a backing track for Dante's Divine Comedy, from all around, came rustling whispers, an innumerable host chanting repetitively, their massed voices getting louder and louder, '*A la luce ... A la luce ...*'

In other words, to the light, to the light ...

I didn't need more encouragement. Unconcerned, my sacks of gold stashed at the base, I scrambled back up the damned assemblage, gagging on raining dust and rubble. Never a thought as to who or what, on which relatives, I might be standing - fear of perpetual interment spurring me on.

I was through, standing in a high corbelled vault, constructed from stone blocks cut on the slant - a technique employed in ancient Egypt to disperse the shock of earthquakes - a high workshop of sorts, set out with white marble tables, some occupied by mummies in a state of dismemberment - limbs separated at the joints, wizened heads from shoulders, bandages strewn. The other slabs occupied with cutting and grinding equipment, pestles and mortars, saws and chisels. Racks lining the walls behind, filled with canopic jars, variously labelled, 'fingers, toes, ears, eyes, sex organs, entrails', and a whole sub-section for brains, 'left hemisphere, right hemisphere, fore brain, reptilian brain', and so on, while others were just filled with grey powder. All that was of but passing interest, however, when compared to the facing stone staircase, lined up with the pavement at my heels, ascending steeply to that opening in the corbelled ceiling above, beyond which I could see dawn breaking through the branches of a bushy cactus swaying in the wind.

Freedom. The mere prospect wiping from mind any resurgent worries for the sacks of gold coins stashed in the darkness below. I only had a few more steps to go before I made it up to top. But then I saw what was moving those branches. Not the wind as I'd presumed, but an enormous bird, distinguished by its leathery scales and an ugly bump at the back of its great beak, the eyes, glinting, concentric circles of doom, focussing on me immobile, in no-man's-land, half way up a staircase of skeletons, going to dust. That was a *tzitzimime*, I was sure. What else could it be? No other bird I knew of with scales instead of feathers. guarding the entrance for Lord Mictlántecuhtli, to Tláltipec –the surface world I'd left so long before. By the size of its great beak and sharp claws, and what had to have been at least a 5-meter wingspan, the pterodactyl, chucamarra, call it what you will, was more than a match for this mere mortal; giving me no option but to retreat and look for another route out.

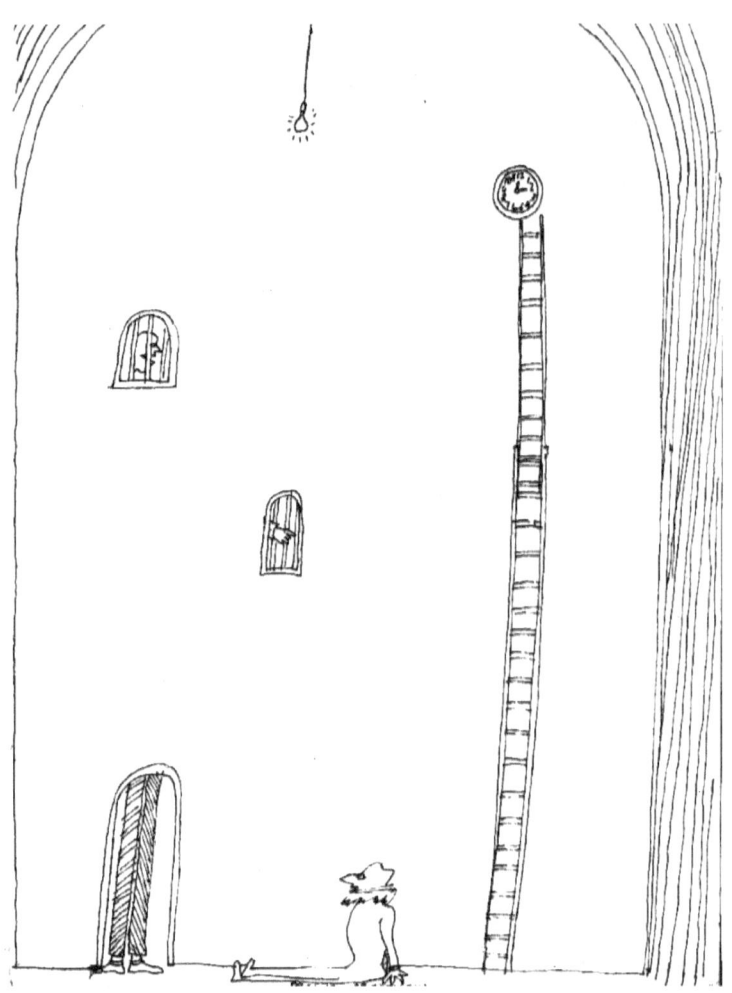

21

THE PRISONER OF CONSCIENCE

Of course, I remembered my cache of gold coins. How could I not when I was like Cortez, sick with gold fever? My mind, however, was rebelling at the thought of returning for the sacks through the circular opening at my feet into the unquiet darkness below. Stress, that's all it was, I reasoned. I'd been so long entombed, I'd developed a profound terror of being buried alive. I was even finding this mortuary workshop hard to endure, what with all these stiffs in bits lying all around. After I'd found another way out to the surface, I reasoned, I would return with a torch. My collection of coins would be safe enough 'till then, camouflaged as they were in the sacks I'd constructed from grey bandages of the same pale tone as that dusty pile, stashed at the base of the midden.

Life, I was rediscovering, is a marvellous thing, crammed full of fascinating distractions. Even the side passages where I found myself, after crawling out of that corbelled mortuary vault, passing under a stone portcullis, like the one leading into the king's chamber in the great pyramid in Giza, were full of surprises. Eerie sounds of cymbals and discordant chanting, that came and went as I explored the turns of what was proving to be a bit of a labyrinth. An overused word in this account, I know, but valid none the less in the context of those interminable echoing long corridors that led only to more of the same. Each, as far as I could make out, with identical proportioned blank doorways regularly spaced at intervals. An architectural style or actual blocked-up doorways, I couldn't tell. Feeling my way along, once more in darkness, wondering if I would ever again see the light. I shouldn't have worried for, around the next corner, half way up the corridor, ruby light was spilling frayed red curtaining. There was sound too, that of a religious service in progress in the room beyond.

I should have held back and stayed where I was, but fascination got the better of me. Would that I had not succumbed and instead tiptoed away from that baleful red light. But curiosity is a powerful urge hard to resist and, besides, that light was as oxygen is to a drowning diver, lost without an airline in the abyssal depths of the Humboldt Trench.

Seeing is believing, but still I couldn't credit what was going on. Through a hole in the red curtains, a view into a hoary past that I thought went out with the first dynasty of pharaohs and their pyramids. Those were ancient Egyptians in there – or at least their Mexican equivalent. Sons of Ra or – since I was looking over the gleaming, sweat-beaded, tonsured heads of Shemites – sons of Shem and grandsons of Noah, suitably robed in sackcloth and shod in sandals, some ringing cymbals others blowing on great horns shaped like griffins raised over their shoulders, all facing a dais directly opposite where a bigwig resplendent in purple robes was positioned between flaming torches on the wall behind, seated on an eagle-winged throne – or were those *tzitzimime* wings? – a pyramidal gold mitre, ornamented by a lidded Horus eye, glittering on his dreadlock-wigged head, indulgently smiling and keeping time to the music with a metronome, the side-to-side swaying of his hand seemed to have them all hypnotised.

Not me, however, for I recognised that face, even though I'd only glimpsed it through a fretwork grill of the confessional. Who else but the Irish priest, Father O'Flaherty.

I thought nothing could possibly have topped that, but I was in for another surprise. Abruptly the snaking hand stopped its metronome back and forth as, simultaneously, the clashing cymbals, atonal horns and discordant chanting ceased. Everything was hushed, even the Shemite brothers seemed to collectively hold their breaths as Father O'Flaherty gestured to the side and, to the accompaniment of clanking chains, a manacled and hooded prisoner was brought forth, dragged on to the dais by a square-shouldered, blue-robed, cleric, with his back towards me.

'Sheriff-at-arms,' Father O'Flaherty commanded, 'Show the prisoner's face!'

That was my second surprise, for when the hood was whipped off, I recognised the face beneath.

'Jaime!' I cried, unable to contain my astonishment and pleasure at seeing my friend alive, after believing him murdered by the baron's mercenaries in Happy Valley.

Then I became aware that the congregation of tonsured heads had as turned as one to stare fixatedly at the red curtain behind which I was hiding.

Although I had a running start, without a light or local knowledge or a floor plan as a guide, I was surely doomed, racing that damned labyrinth with sons of Shem and grandsons of Noah hot on my tail. Never more than then, with my pursuers' torches casting a slippery shine ahead to where I was caught in a dyslexic quandary, faced with a choice of right and left, or was that right or left? Both turns, as far as I could make out, dead ends.

Cul-de-sacs at the end of the rainbow? The other way around, surely? I discovered mine as I fell headlong. Did I trip? Or perhaps I had the demented idea of head-butting my way through. Certainly, I was crazed enough. A heavy stone door swinging open onto saltpetre darkness. No time to wonder where or when as I swung back the hinged slab. Leaning with my full weight against it, fearing to breathe until the muffled sounds of pursuit beyond turned and finally faded.

This much was clear, I was in an old abandoned mine, light leaking the shored roof above, suggesting a way out. Conveniently there was even some furniture, an upturned chair and an old chest lying on its side with the lid open. Items that, when arranged with the chest placed below and the chair stacked on top, served as an impromptu ladder. Affording just enough stability to stand balanced with toes teetering on the seat, just long enough to shoulder up a the heavy flagstone of the floor above and at last push through to Tláltipec ...

Yes, somehow I was back home - the hotel the nearest approximation - in my old room, clutching a clear plastic envelope, which, curiously, when I got up from my knees after thanking divine providence for my deliverance, was laying on the floor before me. Inside was what looked like a certificate embossed with impressive looking seals and bearing my name. This, I had to check out.

First things first, however. I had to evict that sleeping stranger, snoring on my bed, laying with his boots on the sheets and his hat beside him. Bad luck, indicating a death in the house, but for who? I pondered, standing at the foot of the bed, unable to believe my eyes. That was me I was staring at. That insouciant intruder was wearing my face. Parallel realities, I supposed. Somehow, somewhere, I'd blundered into one. For no way was I dreaming this doppelganger.

Congratulations, I thought, sitting down beside myself, a sudden lassitude creeping on. Death or transition? Mine to know and mine to find out – or the other way around? – my last thought as I keeled over.

P'SST SCRIPT
(the Nagual's dream ...)

In the dream I'm awake in my bed beside my sleeping double, who's dreaming of a trial. Because he's my dream body, with all that goes with that, I can see what is going on. However, although we have so much in common, my double and I, we diverge where experiences are concerned. The details of this dream baffle me.

Take this Jaime, the manacled prisoner just delivered into the dock by an armed escort of monks from holding cells below. My twin hero-worships him, yet, from my point of view, the man's a real low-life, a narco-traficante with blood on his hands from his short but meteoric rise from *barrio* hustler to top *pistolero*, trading in death across the border. Perhaps that's a bit strong, for he does have some admirable qualities, not least his fashion sense and chutzpah, but when weighed against his many crimes, he certainly deserves to be arraigned. Although clearly not before an ecclesiastical court of shit-eaters, in the crypt of a cathedral where the repeating vaults of the elaborately carved groined ceiling are supported by tall pillars, splayed at the base, as though rooted. Giving the impression of a petrified forest clearing, shady with tenebrous presences, seeming to emanate from deep stone shelves, tiered around the walls, where the outlines of large lead coffins are faintly apparent in dark recesses.

A detail that my double finds disturbing, wishing, as he does, to expunge all memories of his time in Mictlán. But when faced with all those coffins, he can't, for with the scrying ability that is his special talent, he knows they contain the predecessors of the Master of Proceedings, sitting in judgement on a dais before what is the stoutest pillar of that stone forest. Under his dreadlocked wig and gold-brocaded robes the same Black Friar my twin spoke with in the Confessional, under the mistaken belief that he was a Father' O'Flaharty. A title clearly false, for this is none other than the Pope of Shemites, the belief system that predates all other monotheistic religions, even the ancient Jewish faith – sons of Shem, grandsons of Noah, by direct line, survivors of the first Deluge, awaiting the second Deluge on the sixth millennium since creation in the Town With No Name, in the last unmapped fastness of the Sierra Madre.

But since this is the ecclesiastical Court of the Shemite shit-eaters, even though that is their Pope on the dais, until the conclusion of the trial, his proper form of address is worshipful Lord Horus.

Leaning forward, the Pope addresses a tall and curious black-garbed figure, standing expectantly, back turned to the prisoner in the dock, behind him. 'Prosecutor, before we start, ahem ...' his croaky voice, ratcheted lower, 'By what calendar are we reckoning?'

'The Shemite calendar, worshipful Lord Horus.'

'Long count, I assume?'

The Prosecutor nodded, 'Yes, my worshipful Lord.'

'And the year?'

The Prosecutor riffled his papers. 'Five thousand nine hundred and ninety- nine, worshipful Lord Horus.'

'And, ah, what is that in the, ah, Tzendal calendar?'

The Prosecutor consulted a monk at his side. After a moment he looked up. 'Five sun minus five snake, by Brother Valentine's calculation, worshipful Lord.'

'No time to delay then,' the Pope frowned, 'For the Deluge will soon be upon us.' He paused, allowing the import of weighty words to sink in, before banging his gravel, silencing an outbreak of whispering from the Shemite Black Friars packed into pews at the back of the crypt. 'Order! Order!' I will have order,' he boomed. 'Sergeant-at-arms, is the accused fit to plead?'

'Yes, worshipful Lord Horus,' boomed a voice my twin instantly recognised from behind the dock. Under those blue, ecclesiastical robes, the court officer was none other than Baron Hapsburg – revealed a secret Shemite all along.

'Sergeant-at-arms!' the Pope ordered. 'Swear him in.'

'Worshipful Lord Horus,' the Sergeant-at-arms replied, 'The prisoner declines to swear on the Pentateuch of Noah. He asks to be heard on his own recognisance.'

'So be it,' the Pope intoned. 'Prosecutor, read the charges to the apostate.'

'Yes, worshipful Lord Horus,' the black-cowled Prosecutor responded, reminding my twin of a hooded crow as he hopped, more than stepped, up to the dais. 'Prisoner,' he began, turning to face the dock, 'You are charged with felonious acts; to wit, breaking covenant and peddling salacious lies injurious to the Order. What plead you?'

'I am a *sappatista* of *la revolución*, I do not recognise this court!' the prisoner spat, his voice gaining strength and volume. 'I want nothing more to do with your filthy trade in body parts. I only went along because the mummies were useful for smuggling my *drogas*.'

'And where did you smuggle your, ah, *drugs*?' the Prosecutor said, enunciating the last word as if the mere mention of 'drugs' was a criminal act in itself, implying that the general context of trading in body parts was hardly relevant, if at all.

'You know perfectly well, through your foking tunnels.'

'Where exactly?'

'Below the foking borders, ass wipe.'

'Which borders?' the Prosecutor interjected. 'You must be more specific.'

'Ok, I give you the foking list. Under the foking Rio Grandé, the foking River Jordan, the Red foking Sea, the foking Sea of Marmara, the English foking Channel, the Zuiderzee into foking Euroland, the ...'

'Enough!' the Pope thundered, banging his gravel. 'I warn the accused, any further lewd outbursts and you will forfeit your right to a hearing. Furthermore,' he went on, 'It is not for you to question the supremacy of the Court. You must answer the charges as given. What plead you?'

'Fok off, you foking worshipful foking ass foking wipe.'

'The accused has answered in the affirmative,' the Pope ruled, again banging his gravel. 'Prosecutor, you may resume the interrogation.'

'Thank you, worshipful Lord Horus,' the Prosecutor replied. 'Prisoner, when you swore the sacred oaths, it was incumbent upon you to divulge neither the secrets nor the existence of the Order. Do you remember this?'

'Sure,' the prisoner shrugged. 'So what the fok is this to do with the foking price of pistachio nuts?'

'The accused will answer all questions directly and without elaboration,' the Pope interjected.

'Fok you, too!' the prisoner shouted, grinning up at the dais, receiving a blow to his back of his head from the mailed fist of the Baron, in his capacity as the Sergeant-at-arms, standing behind him.

'You will answer,' the Prosecutor insisted. 'Prisoner, I put it to you that you passed on privileged information concerning the existence of the Order to an outsider.'

'You mean the foking moron reporter from the Notional foking Enquirer.'

'Yes.' The Prosecutor nodded. 'Tell the Court where you met.'

'In Rome, after I finish our little business with brother Señor B of the Brussels Lodge,' Jaime laughed. '*Puta* foking *madre*, I fool the fok good, standing in the foking car park, in red robes with a gold foking crozier in my hand. The stupid fok even kneels and kisses the ring on my foking middle finger, when I introduce myself as "Cardinal Sin", *el ultimo* advisor on Latin American affairs to his Holiness. Which would be true, only it is the wrong pope I am telling him about.' He giggled, 'For every word I say, he pays me in dollars, unlike you *pinché* pigs, who only ever come up with foking pesos. Meaning I always loose in the foking exchange.'

'So you admit the charge?'

'Why not?' Jaime shrugged, inspecting the broken state of his fingernails. 'Your foking wor-shit-ful-foking-Lord-foking-Horus-foking-goat-foking-ass-foking-wipe is going to find me foking guilty anyway,' he added, looking up with a sly grin that seemed to imply he knew something the Pope did not.

'The prisoner's guilt has been demonstrated beyond the shadow of a *tzitizimime* wing,' the Prosecutor resumed. 'By his own admission he has passed privy information beyond the circle, thereby breaking covenant. And in his latest testimony he has gone even further, denying the authority of our worshipful Lord Horus, our Pope and incarnate master, demonstrating complete disdain for the Order. I have no alternative therefore but to demand the ultimate sentence.'

'I thank the venerable Prosecutor,' the Pope intoned ponderously, 'For his excellent summation of the salient points. I find the case so proved, that the accused, in his arrogance, did communicate secrets privy to the Order, thereby imperilling his fellows, for if one is not true to all he cheats them, for they have loved him in all matters and are denied his love.' Again he banged his gravel, silencing a sudden expectant buzz from the back of the Court.

'The prisoner will rise,' Lord Horus continued. 'You have been found guilty. Do you have anything to say before I pass sentence?'

'Fok you, do your foking worst, Don foking O'Flarty! ' Jaime cackled.

'Recorder,' the Pope directed angrily. 'Strike his last response from the record.'

He banged his gravel, silencing a sudden chatter from the tonsured Black Friars. 'Prisoner,' he said, setting an ill-fitting black cap askew on his wigged head, 'You will be taken from here to the Tree of Confinement, there to await your execution. Your end will be slow in coming, I promise, so that you may properly contemplate your many crimes against the Order, before your final judgement by his most supreme majesty of the infernal realms below, whose name must never be mentioned within.'

'Viva Lord Mictlántecuhtli!' Jaime interjected with a joyous yell, shaking manacled fists up at the dias. 'He will fok you!'

'Bind and gag him,' the Pope yelled, almost falling off the dais in his desperation to shut the prisoner up. But both knew it was too late, for the name of the great demon had been uttered within the sanctum. Now, as Jaime might have framed it, the *foking* destruction of the *foking* temple was *foking* assured.

END of Volume II of The Escape From Mictlán Trilogy

More Novels by Will Lorimer, published by Inkistan.com

Spanning worlds, realities, genres and possibilities, this counter factual novel begs the question – *what if* our reality is faux, all history bunkum, and the mind boggling conspiracy outlined within its pages, true? What if our culture is just an aggregation of stories recorded in the Book of Eternity? *What if* all the great scientists and savants are mere story tellers? *What if* this isn't a novel at all, but instead is the factual account of a nerve-racking tour of the multiverse, by way describing where we come from and are headed.

(ON THE RUN IN DREAMTIME
(Two editions, one illustrated)

The unlikeliest duo you'll encounter within the covers of a book or otherwise, Lobo and Frankie are the natural successors to Don Juan, and Carlos Castaneda, with a pinch of Laurel and Hardy for good measure. Lobo is a Swiss-Tibetan-playboy-mystic, who believes that Frank is the Chosen One. A pity then that the Chosen One should turn out to be a lazy, dirty mouthed Scotsman with as much mental clarity as a guinea pig, but Lobo is not deterred. Together they blaze an unstoppable trail across an unsuspecting Australia, in a pristine white falcon UTE – cruising the highways, sneaking the byways, and syphoning off gas pretty much everywhere. From the dives of Kings Cross Sydney, to the wild wastes of flying doctor country, they connive, conspire, and con their way in and out of trouble, in scenarios that Lobo creates to demonstrate the secret teachings of his master in a cave, back in Tibet. Along the road they encounter the gay queen of Melbourne, the gorgeous Renaldo Monte-Video, Nazis hiding out in a Queensland banana plantation when not on the Moon, fat necked outback cops, an aborigine-trans-rights activist, lesbian truckers, hookers and frustrated housewives of the outback.

THE LAST OF THE LUTCHENS

(two editions, one illustrated)

the
Last of the
Lutchens

THE ILLUSTRATED EDITION

Will Lorimer

Britain over the last hundred years, through the eyes of an Anglo-Scots family of dubious lineage, featuring the illusions and obsessions of three generations of the Lutchens, woven together in a genealogical tree rooted in a Scotland which we only thought we knew. Starting in the swinging sixties as the Beatles' first single tops the charts and the Cuban Crisis looms, the narrative tracks back through two world wars to uncover a skeleton in the family closet, before proceeding full circle, to when a national crisis threatens to break-up the disunited family. Will the Lutchens go their separate ways, or patch up their differences? Everything hangs in the balance for the family, and also the British nation state.

THE ESCAPE FROM MICTLÁN TRILOGY
BOOK 1

A prodigal bastard searching for his missing father, a Catholic bishop, instead finds his mother managing the only hotel in the Mexican town with no name, where nothing is as it seems, every day is the Day of the Dead, and the cathedral bells toll 13 at midnight. Even the Police chief has fled following the discovery of a mass grave under the bandstand in the main square, and the only safe place in town is the local cantina, where the barman is the narco-cartel banker. Based on the author's real-life experiences in the remote Sierra Madre of Mexico, A Prodigal Bastard is the first book of the Escape From Mictlan Trilogy. The novel is illustrated with drawings by the Author, many of which are from the year he spent trying to escape from the Town with no name.

BOOK 2

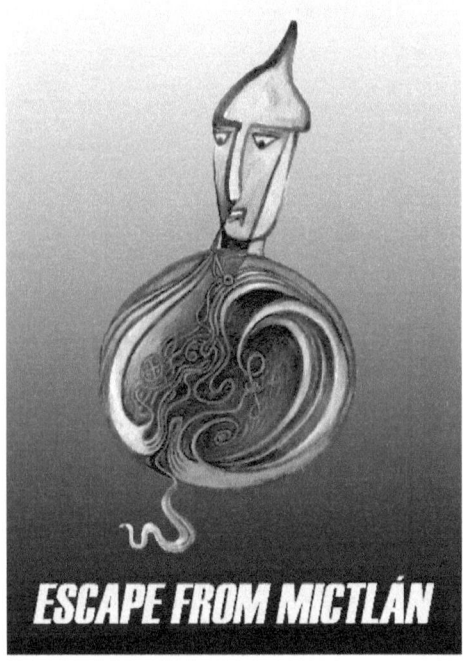

Prodigal bastard's search for his father continues, from the Town with No Name, over the last unmapped mountain range in Mexico, to the Narco HQ, in a hidden canyon, and eventually, into Mictlan, where he finally gets some answers to the questions bugging him ever since the philandering catholic bishop ran out on his life, when he was only 5 years old. Next he has to get out of Mictlán, and his job as the ferryman transporting the dead across the Black River.

BOOK 3

A prodigal bastard returns in a disembodied state to the Town with No Name. Next, he must recover his body, if he is to ever to escape to the world outside.

The Spanish language edition of the Escape from Mictlan Trilogy, in one book.

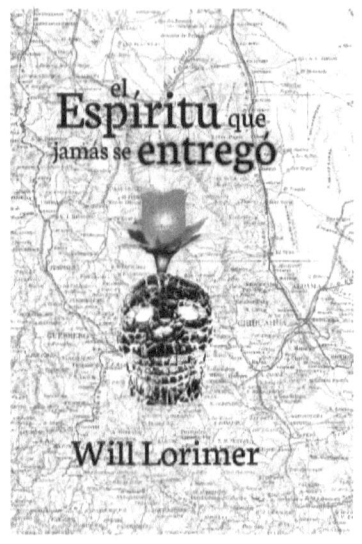

Se trataba de un secreto de su pasado amnésico que ni siquiera su analista de N. Y. era capaz de descifrar, lo que significaba que tenía que ir a México en busca de respuestas, específicamente a un pueblo fantasma en la Sierra Madre, infestada de bandidos, donde su madre lo esperaba en el único hotel del pueblo. En lo recóndito de la Sierra Madre, tras un túnel tallado a través de la cima de una montaña, una de las cinco que rodeaban el lugar como los dedos de una mano, está el pueblo fantasma más extraño de México. Hay un hotel, administrado por una asesina en serie, y justo cruzando la calle, una cantina, administrada por el banquero de un narco-cartel. El pueblo fue fundado en 1495, cuando una banda de conquistadores que, tras la caída de Tenochtitlán, habían estado cazando en las montañas a los últimos guerreros águila aztecas, encontraron plata en las cenizas del fuego de la noche anterior. Eran trece conquistadores, cuyos descendientes gobernaron el pueblo por cuatrocientos años, el más rico de México en su momento, con una tesorería, una casa de moneda, incluso una ópera y por supuesto una catedral, hasta que Pancho Villa y su División del Norte tomaron el pueblo en 1914 y fusilaron a los descendientes de los conquistadores, quienes se llevaron a la tumba la locación del tesoro secreto. Terminada la Revolución, una serie de aventureros, atraídos por la leyenda del Tesoro de la Sierra Madre (algunos decían que había trece tesoros), dinamitó la mayoría de los edificios del pueblo medieval—pero del tesoro, o tesoros, nada nunca se supo. Los nahuas de las remotas montañas piensan que jamás se sabrá, pues es propiedad del Señor de la Muerte, rey del Mictlán, y quien descubra su locación será llevado a uno de los nueve niveles del vasto reino, que yace bajo las minas de plata sepultadas en las montañas. Esta es la historia de una búsqueda de respuestas, entre las cuales está lo que le pasó a un obispo deshonrado, un maldito cabalista enormemente rico, que partió al Mictlán con el secreto de los tesoros, a donde su hijo bastardo tiene que ir, si es que quiere descifrar los enigmas de su pasado amnésico.

WOLFGANG

Book 1 Beware of the Dog)

(The short life and times of WOLFGANG, Laird of Castle Haggard)

Illustrated by the author.

Enfant terrible, a freak of nature. His rise from obscurity to become the Laird of Castle Haggard, following his marriage to Lady Brünhilda Constanze Haggard. His travails restoring the Castle. The strange customs and traditions of the Castle. Beset by demons disturbed by his renovations – a black dog, the Red Duchess, and vengeful ghosts. Betrayed in love - a laird cuckholded. The laird's war against a drug baron and his henchmen. An encounter with Lucifer in a black pit. The riddle of the laird's map of shifting lines and the mystery of the forking paths of the Castle's famous vegetable garden. All this and more recounted in a series of tales, dictated to the laird's secretary, an untrustworthy Inuit, who has an even greater capacity for drugs than the laird himself, which is saying something.

WOLFGANG

Book 2 Beware of the Foby – illustrated

On the run from the authorities, Wolfgang's pursuit of the great novel continues, as he grapples with a world which is much changed since he last left the backwards Kingdom. America is no more, and new powers in the North compete for global domination. Meeting up with his untrustworthy amanuensis in London, he discovers she been playing away, and is back with Skull, his bitter enemy. Next, he learns he is under surveillance by Boreal Intelligence, and an international warrant has been issued for his arrest. Then, he unwittingly crosses an international crime family, and must make amends. Can he survive long enough to write the next volume, let alone complete the great work?

DOG DAYS IN NEW YORK

A collection of short stories of life in Manhattan in the early 1980's. Illustrated by the Author.

MEET THE AUTHOR

Will Lorimer is a multimedia artist. He attended the Scottish School of Hard Knocks and graduated with a PHD in survival strategies.

To find out more about his Art
visit **Inkistan.com**

INKISTAN
.COM

www.ingramcontent.com/pod-product-compliance
Lightning Source LLC
Chambersburg PA
CBHW020248150626
46552CB00020B/715